PAWN OF TERROR

Mark didn't want his new friends to think he was chicken, but he was getting nervous waiting for Greg to break in to the school. When the lock gave, the cadets hastily trooped inside.

"Don't make a lot of noise," warned Greg as they flipped on their flashlights. "At least, not until we find something worth trashing."

"Right," said Warren, a wiry Asian sophomore. "But we can still let them know that we were here." He shook a can of paint, then wrote HMA RULES across four Cooper High lockers.

"Excellent," Greg said. "Now let's go."

The cadets proceeded down the hall until they came upon a glass display case. Mark watched as Greg reached in and pulled out a basketball trophy.

"Wait!" Mark said. "I wouldn't mind breaking up desks or something. But they can't replace these awards."

Greg frowned at him. "That's the point. Come on, man, don't wuss out on us." Even in the dimness, his eyes shone.

Suddenly something chilled Mark's thigh, as if the chess piece Greg had given him had turned to ice in his pocket. Mark's head spun. When the dizziness passed, he was filled with anger. In his hand was a trophy topped with a symbolic atom—probably awarded for somebody's science project. Mark lashed it against the cinder-block wall, then smashed it flat.

Greg grinned

•

NOW OPEN!
THE NIGHT OWL CLUB

Pool Tables, Video Games, Great Munchies,
Dance Floor, Juke Box, *Live* Bands On Weekend.

* * *

Bring A Date Or Come Alone . . .

* * *

Students From Cooper High School,
Hudson Military Academy,
Cooper Riding Academy for Girls
Especially Welcome . . .

* * *

Located Just Outside Of Town.
Take Thirteen Bends Road,
Or Follow Path Through Woods.

* * *

Don't Let The Dark Scare You Away . . .

* * *

Jake and Jenny Demos proprietors
Teen club, no alcohol served.

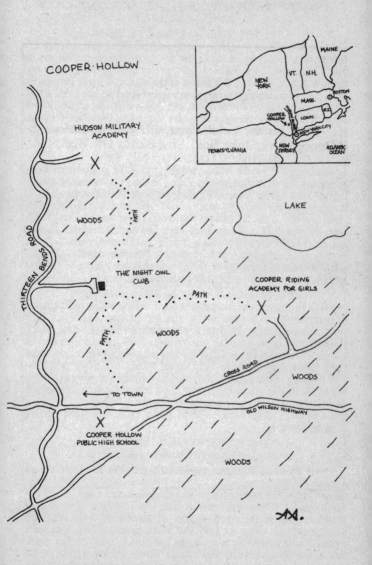

The Nightmare Club

#3: WARLOCK GAMES
Richard Lee Byers

Z·FAVE
KENSINGTON PUBLISHING CORP.

Z*FAVE BOOKS are published by

Kensington Publishing Corp.
475 Park Avenue South
New York, NY 10016

The Nightmare Club series created and edited by Alice
Alfonsi.

First Printing: August, 1993

Printed in the United States of America

For Robert, Doris, Megan, and Nicholas

One

When Mark McIntyre walked into the teen club, the place was jumping. Kids chattered happily, or spun around each other on the dance floor. In the side room, video games buzzed and wailed. One player must have messed up, because the guys clustered around him laughed and jeered.

Nobody said hi to Mark.

It made him feel so lonely that he almost turned around and left. But he knew he'd feel just as lousy sitting by himself in the dorm—or barracks, as the moron instructors called it—so he parked himself at the end of the bar in the back of the room. He figured he'd look less like a social reject perched on one of the stools than if he sat at a booth or table by himself.

The bartender—if that's what you called the person behind the bar, even if she wasn't serving alcohol—worked her way down to him. She was a pretty blonde, probably in her twenties, with big violet eyes. She gave Mark a smile that made him feel a little less down.

"Hi," she said. "I haven't seen you before, have I? I'm Jenny Demos. My father and I own the Night Owl Club."

Mark introduced himself.

9

"You must be a new cadet out at Hudson."

He'd changed out of his gray and navy-blue toy soldier suit before he had left the military academy, so for a second, he wondered how she knew. Then he remembered the haircut the school had made him get. He didn't quite look like a skinhead, but it was close. "Yeah," he sighed.

She lifted an eyebrow. "You don't sound too happy about it."

Mark shrugged. "It's a pain, being the new kid." He ought to know. His father's job made him move so often that Mark had gone to fourteen schools in ten years. And now, with Dad going to Paraguay, Mark had been dumped in the boarding school. He didn't even have his parents around anymore. As far as Mark was concerned, it was a bad joke to send him to an academy with the motto: "We teach leaders of men." He'd never been a leader. Heck, he'd never stayed anywhere long enough to be a follower! He'd always been a stranger, the outsider. "At least if you're the only new *junior*. The other new kids, the sophomore class, hang together, and the older guys hang with the friends they made last year."

Jenny nodded. "I know what you mean, because my dad and I used to travel a lot ourselves. For what it's worth, Cooper Hollow is . . . strange but nice, a thousand times nicer than some places I've seen. I'm sure you *will* make friends, if you just reach out. Did you want to order something?"

"I guess a Coke."

She poured one from the soda dispenser. "There you go. On the house." A boy at the other end of the bar waved an empty glass. "I've got to get back to work. I'll see you in a little while." She bustled away.

As Mark sipped the Coke, he decided that maybe Jenny had given him good advice. If he was lonely, he

10

shouldn't sit and feel sorry for himself, he should try to meet someone. But who? He looked around the club.

And noticed the two girls sitting just a few feet away. One was tall, with frosted curls. The other was short and slim, with a pixieish face and silky brown hair. Somehow, the pair looked nice, not stuck up, and the smaller one was so pretty that Mark would have been interested in meeting her even if he'd already made a thousand friends. He gulped the rest of his drink, pushed his glasses up his nose, got up, and walked over to their table.

"Hi," he said.

The girls looked at him.

He introduced himself. They just kept staring. He blundered on, feeling more awkward by the second. "I, uh, just got to town, and I don't know anybody, and I was wondering if I could sit with you."

The tall girl made a show of looking him up and down. "Well, you don't dress *too* dorky," she said at last. He felt himself redden. She sniffed. "And I don't smell any BO. But you've got that horrible, *horrible* hair, just like the rest of the Hudson Hitler Youth. I don't know if stylish ladies like us—"

"All right," Mark muttered, turning away.

"Wait!" said the pixieish girl. "She's only teasing. Of course you can sit with us. I'm Laurie Frank and my awful friend is Joan Adams."

Mark hastily took a chair. "Thanks. Uh, what school do you guys go to?"

"Cooper High," Laurie said. "And we know where you go. How do you like the Hollow so far?"

"I don't know yet," Mark said. "What do people do for fun around here?"

Laurie frowned, thinking. "Well, of course, there's here, the Nightmare Club . . ."

"I thought it was the Night *Owl* Club," Mark said.

"It is," Laurie said. "But everybody calls it the Nightmare Club because it looks so creepy from the outside. And because the building is supposed to be haunted."

Mark grinned. "Are you kidding me again?"

"Really, that's what the legends say," Joan said. "Probably because so many people have died here. In the late 1700s the place was a tavern where men met to fight duels. In the 1850s it was a stop on the underground railroad, but the couple that ran it went crazy, and tortured and murdered the runaway slaves. In the 1890s it was an orphanage, and a bunch of the children died in a fire. In the 1920s—"

"Don't *ever* give Joan a chance to show how much she knows about something," Laurie said, grinning. "She'll rattle on for hours."

"That's a cruel lie," the tall girl said, smiling back. "It's just that—"

"What are you doing with my sister?" a male voice growled.

12

Two

Startled, Mark twisted in his chair. A beefy guy in a red and white Cooper High varsity jacket was glaring down at him. The newcomer had red, sunburned-looking skin and shoulder-length brown hair that he probably thought made him resemble a rock star. Acne spotted his square jaw.

Laurie scowled. "We're just talking, Barry. Chill before you embarrass yourself, okay?"

"I told you," Barry said, "I don't want you hangin' with guys from Hudson." He sneered at Mark. "Take a hike."

"Why?" Mark asked. "What's the problem?"

"I'm warning you," the hulking boy said. "Go." Kids at nearby tables began to gawk. Some stood up and moved closer.

"Forget it," Mark said. After all, what was Barry going to do about it, pop him in the middle of the teen club?

That was exactly what he did.

Mark was looking at the Cooper High student, but somehow he never saw the punch. One second he was sitting, the next, tumbling, the side of his face stinging. His glasses flew off, and his chair crashed to the floor.

The Hudson cadet scrambled to his feet and raised his fists. Grinning, another guy in a red and white jacket emerged from the mass of spectators, his silver skull earring glinting. "You're toast, rich boy," he said.

Mark's anger turned to fear, a sick, hollow feeling in his stomach. No way could he handle both Cooper High boys at once.

Then two other guys stepped out of the crowd to stand beside him. He was as surprised as he was relieved. He'd seen both kids at Hudson, but they'd never even spoken to him.

"*Three* toy soldiers," Barry said. "Okay, no problem." He shuffled forward to strike. But Mark lunged first, swung, punched him in the gut and doubled him over.

A white-haired man with a beak of a nose shoved through the spectators. Mark guessed he must be Jenny's father. "Stop!" he bellowed.

For some reason, perhaps a trick of the room's acoustics, the shout split the air like a thunderclap. Stunned, the teenagers froze.

"If you fight in here, I'll see you in jail," the old man said, his gray eyes blazing. "If you fight on my *property,* I'll see you in jail. Get out. And don't come back until you learn to behave."

One of the cadets, a chunky, short-legged guy with Ross Perot ears, said, "These jerks started it."

"Out!" Mr. Demos roared. The kid with big ears flinched back. *"Now!"*

Mark hastily picked up his glasses. Then he and the other would-be fighters trudged to the exit, the crowd opening before them. Mr. Demos followed and stood on the stoop, no doubt to make sure they didn't resume their quarrel as soon as they stepped into the night.

Barry sneered at the cadets. "Next time."

"In your dreams," the chunky cadet said.

Barry flipped him off, then he and his friend strode down one of the paths into the woods that separated the Nightmare Club from the rest of Cooper Hollow. The kid with big ears turned to Mark. "McIntyre, right? I remember when Colonel Green introduced you at assembly. I'm Ken Wilson, and this is Greg Tobias."

Greg was tall and thin, with pale skin, black hair, and dark, deep-set eyes that made Mark think of an animal peeking out of a cave. In fact, the guy looked a little creepy, but Mark was too grateful to be put off. He held out his hand. "Thanks, both of you."

"Our pleasure," Greg replied, wrapping his long, white fingers around Mark's. For a moment, his hand felt cold and dry, but the next second, it seemed like anyone else's. "We couldn't let those creeps hurt one of our own."

"I guess we might as well get out of here, too," Ken said. "Go back to the academy."

It occurred to Mark that if he waited where he was, he might be able to talk to Laurie some more. Even though he'd only spent a minute with her, he really liked her. But Mr. Demos might not let him hang around until she came out. And if he walked back to school with Greg and Ken, maybe he could strike up a couple genuine friendships. He could use some. "Sure, let's go," he said.

They set off down a path that ran to the north, their sneakers crunching the first fallen leaves. The sound echoed from the slopes around them. If Mark hadn't known better, he might have thought something was following them.

"So does anybody know what that garbage was all about?" he asked.

Ken said, "Townie guys hate cadets. Especially if we

hit on townie babes."

Mark shoved a pine branch out of his path. The needles pricked his hand. "Why?"

Ken shrugged. "I don't know. Maybe because they think we look stupid playing army, which I guess we kind of do. Or because our families have enough money to send us to private school, and most of theirs don't."

"In other words, they're jealous," Greg said. "And they should be."

Ken said, "I don't know about that. But both years I've been here, there's been trouble. Fights. Practical jokes. That kind of stuff."

Greg smiled. "At orientation, the colonel told us new cadets to uphold Hudson's traditions, didn't he, Ken?"

"Yeah," Ken said.

"Then this year, why don't the three of us, and maybe some others we're sure we can trust, take care of the pranks?"

"I don't know," Ken said. "I cut some classes last year, and the instructors came down on me hard. I don't really want to get into more trouble this year."

"Come on," Greg said, "those townies tried to beat up Mark, two-on-one. We *owe* them. And it'll be fun. You're in, aren't you, Mark?"

Mark said, "I don't know." He didn't particularly want to get into trouble either, and perhaps because he'd managed to hit Barry back, he wasn't quite as mad anymore. "What—"

Greg's black eyes glittered, and suddenly Mark's head began to throb. Suddenly he was reliving the shock of being sucker-punched, and the stab of fear when the kid with the skull earring joined the fight. His rage surged back full force. "I mean, yeah, I'm in," he said.

16

"See?" Greg said. *"Mark's* not chicken." He gripped Ken's shoulder. "Come on, man. We need you. Besides, now you know too much. If you won't join the team, we'll have to kill you." He grinned. His long fingers squeezed.

A chill breeze gusted, and Mark shivered. A cloud oozed in front of the crescent moon. For a heartbeat, Ken's round face looked slack and dazed. Maybe it was a trick of the wavering light.

"Well . . . okay," the stocky senior said, blinking.

"Great!" Greg said. "You know, if we're forming a secret brotherhood, we ought to do it right. Like in the movies. Have tokens to show who belongs." He reached in his pocket and brought out two figurines.

Mark stepped closer to inspect them. They were wooden carvings the soft gray color of a Hudson uniform. One was a turreted tower, and the other was a warrior armed with a spear and shield.

"A rook and a pawn," Ken said. "You carry a chess set in your pocket?"

Greg said, "I like to play, so why not? From now on, carry these with you."

Mark thought the idea was kind of childish, but if it would make Greg happy, what the heck. He took the pawn, and Ken accepted the castle. "I guess we can call ourselves the Chessmen," the chunky senior said.

"I like it," Greg said. "And I think we should start our reign of terror tonight. Meet me on the rifle range an hour after lights out."

Three

Mark crouched in the bushes beside the one-story brick building that was Cooper High. His palms were sweaty and his heart thumped. Greg's screwdriver scraped in the crack between the door and the jamb.

An hour earlier Mark had sneaked out of the dorm and down to the parade ground, where he saw that Greg had already recruited two more Chessmen. The tall, pale sophomore had passed out hammers, hatchets, pry bars, flashlights, and cans of spray enamel that he'd borrowed from the custodian's workroom, then the cadets hopped the wall and walked into town.

Slipping through the deserted streets had been fun, but once they reached Cooper High, Mark started getting nervous. After all, the cadets were trying to break into a public building. If somebody caught them, they'd be in real trouble. He wished they could give it up, but he wasn't quite willing to suggest it. He didn't want his new friends to think he was chicken.

"Why don't we bust a window?" Stan, a junior with a bristly red crewcut, asked. He sounded edgy; Mark was glad that at least he wasn't the only one.

"Somebody might hear," Greg said. "Or come along and see it afterward. I think I'm getting this, just keep your pants on." He murmured something under his breath. The door clicked. "There!" Gripping the handle, he pulled it open.

The cadets hastily trooped inside, into a locker-lined hallway. Flashlights clicked on. Circles of white light swooped about.

Greg pulled the door shut. "Don't make a lot of noise," he warned. "At least, not until we find something worth trashing."

"Right," said Warren, a wiry Asian sophomore. "But we can still let them know that we were here." He shook a can of paint, then wrote HMA RULES across four lockers. The hiss of the spray seemed loud in the stillness. The smell stung Mark's nose.

"Cool," Greg said. "But you ought to really dis them. Get personal."

Warren grinned. "You got it." He wrote a dirty remark about Cooper High girls, then drew a rude picture to go with it. Watching, Mark felt ashamed and excited at the same time. Ashamed because he didn't like the thought of a nice girl like Laurie having to see something so nasty, and excited because it was fun to be a part of something forbidden.

"Excellent," Greg said, slapping Warren on the shoulder. "Now let's go." The Chessmen proceeded farther into the school, Warren and Stan occasionally pausing to paint more graffiti.

Near the school's main entrance the cadets found an oil painting of pioneers building log cabins. On the wall opposite it was a display case crammed with plaques and trophies.

Greg said, "This is it."

Stan shook his paint can, then sprayed a four-letter word across the bottom of the painting. Greg tried to open the case, but the glass door wouldn't slide. Mark expected him to jimmy it, but instead he impatiently rapped it with the back of his fist. The glass shattered.

Ken gaped. "Jeez! Did you cut yourself?"

Greg smiled and held up his unmarked hand. "No." He reached into the case and pulled out a cup with a little bronze basketball player on top of it.

Mark didn't know he was going to speak until the word tumbled out of his mouth. "Wait!"

Greg frowned at him. "What is it?"

"Well . . . look. I wouldn't mind breaking up desks or something like that, because they can get more. But this picture and the trophies are different. They can't replace them."

"That's the point," Greg said. "We want to really tick them off."

"I know," Mark said, "but—"

Greg said, "Come on, man, don't wuss out on us. The rest of us are only here because people messed with *you*. You still want to get even, don't you?" Even in the dimness, his dark eyes shone.

Something chilled Mark's thigh, as if the chess piece he held in his pocket had turned to ice. His head spun. When the dizziness passed, he was angry again. In his hand was a trophy topped with a symbolic atom—probably awarded for somebody's science project. He lashed it against the cinder-block wall. The base snapped off and fell to the floor. Mark dropped the cup and stamped it flat.

The other Chessmen cheered and started trashing the rest of the awards. Tools rose and smashed down. The chopping and hammering echoed.

In two minutes, all the trophies and plaques were ruined. Grinning, his chest heaving, Ken asked, "What's next?"

"I don't know," Greg said, looking around. "I wonder—"

One of the doors that made up the school's main entrance clicked. Someone was unlocking it. Fearing it was the police, the Chessmen bolted back the way they'd come.

A fast runner, Mark plunged ahead of his friends, then skidded around a corner. A flashlight beam slashed through the darkness before him. Sure enough, a policeman had come through one of the exits ahead, blocking the cadets' escape route.

"Hey!" the cop shouted. He charged forward.

Mark scrambled back around the corner. The other Chessmen almost piled into him. The boys could hear footsteps thumping behind them.

"There's another one in front of us!" Mark gasped.

"Then we're surrounded!" Ken said. "They got us!"

"No," Greg said coldly. He gripped his screwdriver like a dagger.

He wants to *attack* the cops, Mark thought in amazement.

Greg looked at his companions. If he really *did* want them to fight, he must have understood from their frightened faces that they wouldn't do it, because he scowled, opened a classroom door, and said, "In here!"

The Chessmen scrambled inside. "The windows!" Mark said.

"They don't look like they open wide enough," Greg replied. He shoved the other cadets into the corner. "Get down. Squeeze together. Hold your chess pieces in one hand and touch *my* hand with the other."

It sounded nuts, but Mark was scared enough to go along with almost anything. He did as Greg had ordered, and the other cadets did, too.

Greg bowed his head and murmured something under his breath. Something sprinkled on the back of

Mark's hand. In the dark, he couldn't see it, but it felt like hair. The air turned cold.

The door swung open. A flashlight beam flicked across desk tops and green chalkboards, then the mass of huddled boys. Mark felt one of his companions shudder.

The policeman turned and closed the door behind him.

"I don't believe it," Ken whispered. "The light was *on* us. How could he not see us?"

"Quiet!" Greg said. "Nobody move." After a while, he crept to the door and peeked out. "Hall's clear. Come on."

The Chessmen skulked on down the corridor. Periodically they heard the policemen's voices echoing through the school, but they made it to an exit without sighting the cops again.

Once outside, they ran for all they were worth. Finally, when they'd put several blocks between themselves and the school, Greg held up his hand. Everyone stumbled to a halt.

"Yes!" Stan shouted, punching at the air like a member of Arsenio's studio audience. "Yes, yes, yes!"

Warren threw back his head and howled like a wolf.

Mark felt elated, too. Why not, they'd done what they'd set out to do, and had a narrow escape. But something was nagging at him. In fact, Mark was surprised he was the only one who seemed to be curious. He looked at Greg. "What did you do back there?"

Greg's eyes widened as if he was surprised that any of them would question him. Then he smiled sheepishly, the expression looking somehow unnatural on his narrow, thin-lipped face. "Don't make me say."

"Come on," Ken said. "I'd like to know, too."

"Oh, all right," the black-haired sophomore said. He scratched his head. "When I was a little kid, my friends and I made up a magic spell to turn invisible. With those cops breathing down our necks, it popped back into my head, and I was so panicky, I tried it. Pretty retarded, huh?"

"Totally," Ken said, grinning.

Except that Greg was the only one of us who *didn't* seem scared, Mark thought. And the magic really did hide us.

Except no, of course it hadn't. There wasn't any such thing as magic. The cop was just blind.

And since that was so, Mark couldn't understand what was bothering him. He tried to forget his anxieties and enjoy the rush of the Chessmen's victory.

Four

The Nightmare Club was a shuttered cube of a building. Only one light burned outside, a dim blue bulb over the door. Dead, crooked trees clustered around the structure like skeletal hands fondling a gravestone. When the breeze blew, their bare branches scraped along the grimy brick walls.

At night, Mark thought, the place really does look haunted. He shivered.

"I hope Mr. Demos lets us in," Ken said.

"Me, too," Mark replied. They stepped onto the porch and opened the door.

It was Saturday evening, and even though it was still early, the teen club was busy. Delivering burgers to a table near the door, Mr. Demos glared when the cadets came in, but didn't speak. Mark felt himself relax.

The cadets claimed a booth on the wall. Mark said, "Well, he didn't kick us out, but he sure gave us the eye."

"He always looks at kids that way," Ken said. He glanced around, lowered his voice. "But for a second, when we first came in, I felt like *everyone* was staring at me."

"Well, they aren't," Mark said. "Nobody knows who broke in, so be cool."

Jenny Demos, smiling and friendly as if there hadn't been any trouble last night, came to take their order. After she left, Ken said, "It was all pretty weird, huh?"

"Yeah."

"Do you think we're mean, rotten people?"

Mark shrugged. "I don't know. If you thought it was bad, why didn't you back me up when I tried to stop it?"

"I didn't think so *then*. It was like I was temporarily insane."

Mark nodded. "I know what you mean. Looking back, it seems like a dream. Like there are two of me, the one that got mad and ran wild last night and the one I usually am. But look. It's over. We didn't get caught, and we didn't kill anybody. So there's no point beating ourselves up."

Ken said, "I guess you're right. After all, those townie creeps had it coming." He grinned. "And it was fun."

"What was?" a girl's voice asked.

Mark and Ken jerked around. Laurie was standing beside their booth.

Mark's heart pounded. How much had she heard? Then he realized from her smile that she couldn't have heard much at all.

"The rifle range," he lied. "I never shot a gun before. It's fun."

"Oh. Can I join you?" she asked.

He peered at her. "Well, you aren't *too* ugly." He sniffed. "And just a little stinky. But —"

She laughed. "No fair. It was Joan who put you through that, not me."

"Sure, sit," Mark said, scooting over. "Barry will

have a harder time knocking me out of a booth."

"He's not here anyway," Laurie said. "He went to a movie." She slid onto the red-leather seat. Her leg brushed his. The touch tingled.

The three teenagers chatted for a minute. Then Ken said, "I'm going to see if anybody's playing MegaCity Marshal." He got up and headed for the game room.

Laurie brushed back her brown hair and smiled. "I like him, but I'm glad he left. It makes it easier to apologize for my brother. Is your face okay?"

Mark touched the bruise. "Yeah. It just stings a little. Look, you don't have to apologize for Barry, but can you explain him? I know he doesn't like cadets, but jeez, he sucker-punched me for, really, no reason. Is he Cooper's official psycho, or what?"

Laurie sighed. "Believe it or not, he's really a nice guy. At least he used to be. Last year, he dated this girl named Traci Elmore. He really liked her, but she dumped him for a cadet named Wes Lombard. Wes had kind of a bad reputation. Supposedly, he was into drugs. One night, he took Traci walking in the woods, and they never came out."

Mark frowned in puzzlement. "What do you mean, they never came out?"

"Nobody ever saw them again. Some people thought they eloped. Others thought that Wes went crazy, murdered Traci, hid her body, and ran away." Laurie's lips quirked into a momentary smile. "Some even thought one of the Hollow's spooks got them. Anyway, ever since they vanished, Barry has hated cadets. He's afraid that if I hang around with any, something will happen to me."

"That's stupid," Mark said, "but maybe I can understand why he feels that way. If he thinks he's protecting you, maybe he isn't as much of a creep as I thought."

26

Jenny brought Cokes and a basket of onion rings. "Help yourself," Mark told Laurie. "Ken won't mind."

She picked up an onion ring, shook salt on it, and bit it in two. "Hot!" She chewed awkwardly, trying to keep the food from burning her mouth. "Now that I think about it," she said after swallowing, "there's a little more to Barry's part of the story. Last year, he hated cadets, but he wouldn't have done what he did last night. But this year, he *really* hates them. You'd think time would help him get over Traci, but it seems like it's done the opposite. And some of her other friends are the same way. Funny, huh?"

"And sad."

"I wish some of you cadets hadn't wrecked our school's trophies. Did you hear about that?"

Feeling guilty, Mark nodded.

"That's going to make everybody's hard feelings even worse," said Laurie.

For a moment, Mark wanted to confess what he'd done. But he couldn't rat on his new friends. He'd just have to be incredibly nice to Laurie and make amends without her knowing that that's what he was doing. "I'm sorry that happened," he said.

"Thanks," she said. "You're nice to say so, considering how Cooper guys treated you."

Mark felt another twinge of shame. He ignored it. "Then would you like to go out some time?"

She smiled. "Even though my brother's the Terminator?"

He nodded.

"Then yes."

27

Five

Mark got back to Hudson after lights out. He'd had so much fun with Laurie that he'd had trouble tearing himself away. As he moved along the seven-foot wall, he was grateful that Ken had shown him and the other Chessmen how to sneak in and out of the compound.

The best place to do it was halfway down the west side of the enclosure, where a stand of oaks growing just inside blocked the view from the academy's main building. When Mark reached that point, he moved a couple of paces away from the wall, preparing to run, jump, and scramble over.

Then he heard rapid footsteps thudding on the other side.

Mark wondered what was happening. Had the rest of the Chessmen set out on another late-night adventure, or was this another bunch of cadets? And whoever it was, why were they making noise before they cleared Hudson property?

Two hands clutched the top of the wall. A teenage boy with longish blond hair and wearing a brown leather jacket swung himself over and dropped. Mark could see the boy wasn't a cadet. He looked up, saw Mark, and gaped.

"Who are you? And what are you doing here?" Mark challenged.

The boy lunged, arms outstretched to push Mark out of the way.

Mark tried to twist aside, but he was a second too slow. Hands thumped him and he stumbled backward, nearly falling. His attacker ran on.

Angry now, Mark started to dash after him, then he heard noises, that sounded like other guys were about to jump the wall. He couldn't fight them all, so he crouched behind a pine tree.

An instant later, several other teenagers hurdled over the enclosure, Barry Frank and the kid with the skull earring among them. They hooted and howled, then ran toward town.

Mark waited a few seconds to be sure there were no stragglers, then he clambered over the wall himself.

Across a wide expanse of yard stood the academy's four-story main building. Two wings extended at angles from the dome-topped central section. It looked like a courthouse or a statehouse. Ordinarily, at this hour, the exterior would have been almost as dark as the outside of the Nightmare Club. But for some reason many of the windows were lit. Figures stumbled out of the exits and toward the front of the building. Mark could hear them babbling excitedly, even from where he stood.

Using trees and bushes for cover, he skulked forward until he could slip into the milling, chattering crowd. Then he pushed ahead to see what all the commotion was about.

In front of the school's main entrance stood a bronze statue of a bearded soldier with a pegleg. According to the inscription on the granite base, it was an effigy of Oswald Cooper, who'd commanded the local regiment in the Civil War. He'd lost his limb at the Battle of Antietam, then founded the school in 1867.

Now the statue lay on its back, beside a raw, square indentation where its pedestal had been embedded in the ground. Oswald's face had been so fiercely beaten that it hardly seemed to have eyes or a nose anymore, while further assaults had dented and twisted his body. Four-letter words, spray-painted in red and white, defaced the carving on the statue's base. Colonel Green, the head of the school, a tall, bald man with a long, pointed nose and round, steel-rimmed glasses, glared down at the wreckage, quivering. He looked angry enough to kill somebody.

Even though a Cooper High kid had manhandled him *again,* Mark was now more puzzled than angry. Even disturbed. Maybe everyone else thought the vandals had somehow unlocked the academy's wrought-iron gate, driven a car inside, used it to push or pull Oswald over, then hammered him with tools. But he'd seen Barry and his friends flee on foot, with their hands empty. And he couldn't imagine how a few kids with no tools could topple and mangle something so heavy.

Someone tapped him on the shoulder. He jumped and spun around.

Behind him stood Greg, dressed in pajamas and a plaid bathrobe. His black hair stood out from his head in spikes and tufts. He smelled slightly rank, as if he'd been sweating in his sleep. "Sorry," he said, "I didn't mean to startle you." He lowered his voice. "Chessmen meeting tomorrow evening. Rifle range, seven o'clock."

30

Six

The sun was setting behind the wooded hills west of the Hollow, staining the sky pink and gold and casting long shadows across Hudson's well-tended lawns. The frisbee floated through the air. Mark ran, jumped, caught it, and spun it Ken's way.

The game of catch was supposed to keep people from realizing that the eight Chessmen—Greg had recruited three more during the day—had assembled in the field to talk privately. As Ken snatched the flying disk out of the air, the black-haired sophomore said, "Here's the situation: Cooper High burned us good last night. We have to burn them back."

"I'm up for it," Cliff, a junior with braces, said.

"Me too," said Bob, a lanky black sophomore, wearing a Malcolm X cap.

Mark sighed. He didn't want to be the one who opposed what everyone else wanted, who sounded chicken, but he didn't see any other choice. "Maybe we shouldn't," he said. "At least not yet. The police know there's been vandalism two nights in a row. So they're sure to be watching for more tonight." The frisbee flew from Ken to Warren.

"So what?" Greg said. "If we use our heads, they won't catch us."

31

"You can't be sure of that," Mark replied. "Do we really want to risk getting our butts in trouble, just because somebody trashed old Oswald? Did anybody here actually *like* the thing?"

Greg's eyes narrowed. Mark again felt as if the chess piece in his pocket were a piece of ice. "That doesn't matter. The statue's a symbol of our school. When somebody attacks something like that, you have to hit back. Otherwise, they'll think you're afraid of them, and keep on taking shots at you forever, just for fun."

Mark felt dizzy. Wishing someone else would help him argue against Greg, he looked around the circle. Everyone else was nodding at what the pale sophomore had said. It was almost like they were hypnotized.

Mark struggled to put his jumbled thoughts into words. "Look, if we want to get these guys, there's a simpler way. I was out past curfew last night. I saw them running away. I can point them out to the police."

Greg stared at him. For a moment, Mark thought he saw webs of wrinkles creeping out from the sides of the sophomore's mouth and the corner of his left eye. But no one else seemed to notice it, so he supposed it must be a trick of his blurring vision. "That's a bad idea," Greg said. "Because it could get *you* in trouble. Because it would only be your word against theirs. And most importantly, because we want to show Cooper High that we're smarter, braver, and tougher than they ever dreamed of being, so they'll be scared to mess with us again. And you can't do that by snitching to somebody. You have to fight your own fight. Am I right?"

Mark shook his head. "I—I don't know."

Greg's eyes bored into him. "Remember how that

32

guy decked you when you weren't looking? And how he and his buddy were going to double-team you? Aren't you still mad?"

Mark realized he was. The anger was like a tide rising inside him, drowning his doubts and fears. He struggled futilely to resist it.

"Think how much fun Friday night was," Greg continued. "How good it felt to get even. Wouldn't you like to feel that rush again?"

"Yeah," Mark admitted. "Okay. I'll do it."

Dave, a sophomore who was breaking Hudson's dress code by wearing his striped uniform pants with British Knights and an Alice in Chains tee-shirt, yelled, "All right, Mark!" The other Chessmen smiled. Their approval made Mark feel warm inside.

Greg said, "We'll meet here again at midnight."

Seven

Crouching behind the maple, Mark felt dazed and feverish. What am I doing here? he wondered. I don't want to trash Laurie's school.

He looked at Ken kneeling behind the tree next to his. The chunky senior grinned at him. The joy in his smile washed away Mark's momentary doubts, brought his own euphoria flooding back. It was thrilling to range through the night with friends. To do something risky. To strike back at the enemies they hated.

An engine growled to life. The blue and white police car in front of Cooper High finally rolled down the street, turned a corner, and vanished.

"Come on!" Greg said. The Chessmen leaped up, dashed toward the rear of the school, where no one could see them from the street.

"What now?" Mark asked. "Break in again? They might have new alarms—"

Greg frowned as if the other cadets weren't supposed to think, just wait for him to tell them what to do. "I thought of that," he said. "So we'll wreck something out here." He looked around. "There." He loped toward Cooper's football field. The other Chessmen trotted along behind him.

The level expanse of grass was black in the darkness. The chalk lines glimmered faintly. The cool autumn breeze rolled a paper cup clicking along the tarmac beneath the stands.

Stan waved a mallet at the goal posts. "We could tear those down."

"We could," Greg said. "But it wouldn't be much trouble for them to put up new ones. And we're here to give them trouble." He turned toward the bleachers. "So let's wreck these."

The other boys gaped. Except for their plank seats and foot rests, the stands were made of steel, and mounted in concrete. Ken said, "You're kidding."

"No," Greg said. "Our statue was big and heavy, and the Cooper jerks knocked it over. Are they tougher than us?"

"No!" Cliff said.

"No," Mark agreed. "But Oswald wasn't anywhere near as big and heavy as these stands."

Greg smiled. "Do you know why soldiers don't march in step when they cross a bridge?"

The question caught Mark by surprise. He blinked. "Yeah. Because if they did, the vibration could shake it down."

"Right. And what if we shake the bleachers, all pushing and pulling at the same time?"

Mark shook his head. "It won't work. There aren't enough of us."

Greg said, "We're the best guys from the best school in New York state. We can do *anything,* if we believe in ourselves and work as a team. Look, just try, okay? Think how freaked out these Cooper creeps will be when they see the remains. They'll never hassle a cadet again."

35

"What the heck," Ken said. He dropped his hatchet. It clinked on the pavement. "Let's give it a shot."

Mark shrugged. "Okay. If that's what it takes to convince you."

Greg positioned the cadets along one side of the bleachers. Each gripped a piece of the frame in both fists. "Push! Pull!" Greg chanted. "Push! Pull!"

Even though Mark was certain the effort was going to fail, he didn't hold back. He'd said he'd try, and he did. He hurled his weight back and forth in time to the rhythm. The steel cut into his hands.

And before long, the violent motion became pleasant. It fed his excitement, and his sweet, glowing hatred of Barry and his friends.

Suddenly, he heard shivering singing through the frame. Mark told himself it was only the vibration they were trying to create, but it felt more like a weird energy. It seemed to buzz from one Chessman to the next, somehow making each of them stronger.

And something *was* making them stronger. He could feel it in his own muscles. To his right, something ripped. He turned his head. Ken's tee-shirt had split up the back. If Mark hadn't known better, he would have sworn that the other cadet's body was actually changing shape, the shoulders broadening and the forearms thickening.

The Chessmen bellowed with each shove and pull. The bleachers squealed, groaned, and finally shrieked.

The section of frame Ken was pushing came apart. Off-balance, he stumbled forward. Mark grabbed his arm and jerked him back, just as a third of the stands came crashing down.

Unfazed as a rain of metal and wood fell mere inches from their bodies, the cadets cheered, danced, and high-fived each other. Then they dashed around the wreckage to attack the remaining bleachers. The second section collapsed more quickly, and the last tumbled in less than a minute.

As Mark stood panting, his muscles aching and his heart pounding, it seemed to him that not just Ken but all of the Chessmen looked different. Stan's hands seemed too large. Warren's mouth was wider, his forehead lower. And Greg was shorter and even thinner, as if he'd shriveled inside his clothing.

Mark blinked stinging sweat out of his eyes, took off his glasses and wiped them with his shirt. When he put them back on, everyone *still* looked different, but he couldn't pinpoint the changes anymore. He told himself they were just his imagination.

"Let's book," Greg said. "The cops have to be on their way back. We made enough noise to wake up Canada."

They were turning to go when an odd sound came from nearby. Something was bleating.

The cadets pivoted. Thirty feet away stood a low-roofed shed. Mark had glanced at it before, but hadn't noticed the chicken-wire fence, or the trough and bucket by the door.

Greg smiled. "Maybe we can stay a *little* longer."

The cadets hurried to the shed, then stooped to peer inside. No doubt frightened by the tumult of the collapsing bleachers, a black and white goat stood against the far wall. Mark realized it must be Cooper's mascot. The school team was the Red Devils, so a horned, cloven-hoofed, and bearded animal was the best living symbol they could find.

Greg reached into the enclosure, grabbed the goat by one of its horns, and pulled it out. The other cadets swarmed around it.

Shocked out of his elation, Mark realized they were

going to kill the animal! He opened his mouth to beg them not to, but before he could get the words out, Stan swung his hammer. In another instant, all the boys were striking.

Even after the animal was killed, the cadets wouldn't leave it alone. Stan and Bob finger-painted their faces with its blood. Cliff cut off an ear. Ken chopped off a hoof, and Dave, grunting and red-faced, struggled to break loose a horn.

Mark doubled over and vomited.

Eight

Monday passed in a kind of blur. Dazed with shame, Mark had moments when he couldn't believe the events of the previous night had really happened. Then he'd visualize the goat's kicking hooves and rolling eyes. His stomach churned and he nearly threw up again.

Try as he might, he couldn't understand how a bunch of supposedly normal teenagers could torture and kill a helpless, harmless animal. If he hadn't known it was impossible, he might almost have imagined they were all turning into monsters.

That afternoon, Colonel Green called a special assembly, where he denounced the "outrages" of the weekend, and threatened all vandals with expulsion and criminal prosecution. As Mark squirmed in his seat, it occurred to him that the principal at Cooper High was probably giving his students the same lecture.

But if he did, it didn't work. In the middle of the night, something boomed. When Mark stumbled to the barracks window, he saw that four of the cars in the parking lot were burning.

He cringed, because he was sure Colonel Green's threats didn't matter; now Greg would want the

Chessmen to strike at Cooper again.

The call to battle came shortly after supper the following evening. Mark was lying on his bunk, feeling punchy from lack of sleep but trying to study his trig assignment anyway, when Stan stuck his head in the door. "Meeting right away," he murmured. "In the natatorium." He hurried down the hall, no doubt to tell other Chessmen.

All right, Mark thought grimly. This time I have to convince them to stop. Before somebody gets hurt. Or before we get caught, and Laurie decides she doesn't want anything to do with me. After what's happened, surely some of the others already want to quit.

But could he convince them? Or would Greg manage to dominate him again?

The cadet grimaced, disgusted at his timidity. At his overactive imagination. Greg was just a kid, not a supervillain out of some comic book. He was persuasive, a natural leader, but he couldn't control people like they were puppets.

But Mark also knew nothing could explain the strange things that kept happening. Like becoming invisible to the police, and the abnormal strength the Chessmen gained to tear down the bleachers. And the cold spot that sometimes chilled his thigh.

Mark's eyes narrowed. Suppose Greg *was* a superguy, or a magician of some kind, and the chess pieces he'd told the other cadets to keep in their pockets were props that helped him control them — the strings on the puppets, so to speak? And suppose that when they were working, they sometimes turned cold. *That* would account for the weird chill he sometimes felt.

More crazy thinking. He had to stop, or he'd get himself too spooked to go to the meeting. On the other hand, now that the idea had occurred to him,

40

Mark knew he didn't want to carry his pawn around any longer. He fished it out of his pocket, dropped it in a dresser drawer, and walked to the pool. Glancing around to make sure no one was watching, Mark slipped through the door.

With the lamps on the walls turned off, the natatorium felt like a cave. The round lights in the bottom of the pool cast glimmering ripples on the ceiling. The other Chessmen were clustered around the diving board. Mark was surprised to see that despite Colonel Green's warning, there were two new recruits.

Mark sat on the tile floor beside Ken. The surface was damp.

"And now we're all here," Greg said, still wearing his uniform even though the day's classes were over. He sat on the diving board, his long legs dangling and his white face even more ghostly in the glow of the luminous water. "So let's get started. We all know what the Cooper High geeks did last night. Obviously, our raids haven't yet convinced them to leave us alone. But I think I know what will. If it doesn't bother them when we tear up their school, we'll target the creeps themselves. Burn *their* cars. Beat *them* up. We know one of their names, Barry Frank, already, and Mark's seen most of their faces, so we won't have any trouble tracking them down."

"Hold it," Mark said. Everyone turned and looked at him. "We can't go on with this."

"Like heck we can't!" one of the new recruits, a chubby kid with a squeaky voice, said. "They nuked my 'vette!"

"That's rough," Mark said, "but trashing somebody else's car won't bring it back. Didn't you guys hear what Colonel Green said? Do you want to get kicked out of school? Sent to jail?"

Greg stared at Mark. The junior could feel the

41

weight of that gaze, but so far at least, it wasn't making him feel stupid or feverish the way he had before. "No one will catch us," Greg said soothingly. "We're smarter than Green. Or the cops. Or anybody." Other cadets murmured in agreement.

"Look," Mark said, "even if they wouldn't catch us—and we don't know that—this is getting crazy. Doesn't anybody else feel bad about what we did to that poor goat?"

Dave shrugged. "It was just an animal."

"Cooper's animal," Stan said with a sneer.

Mark turned to Ken. "Tell them, man. Maybe they'll listen to you."

The stocky senior shrugged. "Sorry, but I'm on their side." Mark gaped at him. Ken had been ashamed of trashing the awards, so how could he not regret what had happened Sunday night? "Cooper hit us, so we have to hit them harder. If we didn't, we'd be losers. Wimps. I think you're going soft on us because of Laurie. You should dump her and find a girl from the Riding Academy."

Mark shook his head in bewilderment. "You're as nuts as the rest of these guys. Don't you remember, you *liked* Laurie. You left the booth to give me a chance to be alone with her. Anyway, she's got nothing to do with this."

"He's dating a girl from Cooper High?" Warren asked.

Ken nodded. "Laurie Frank."

"Barry's *sister!*" Warren said. "Jeez, no wonder he wants us to wimp out! He's a stinking *spy!*"

Mark said, "I am not!" Then several of the Chessmen lunged at him.

He knocked aside a grasping hand, jumped up to run for the door. A fist clutched his ankle, and he slammed back down on the tile. The impact knocked

42

the wind out of him.

Leering cadets loomed over him, looking just as they had when they ripped the goat apart. Some of their eyes seemed to shine; he could tell the colors even in the gloom. Six guys grabbed him, lifted him, and carried him toward the pool.

Mark thrashed wildly. He thought he could feel a trace of the inhuman might that had demolished the bleachers in his captors' iron grips, but he couldn't muster a shred of it himself.

The back of his skull bounced against the edge of the pool, half stunning him. His attackers plunged his head and shoulders under the surface of the water. The impact tore his glasses off.

He struggled. Still he couldn't break free. Pressure began to build inside his chest and throat.

They're just trying to scare me, he told himself. Any second, they'll pull me up. But they didn't.

A tall, thin figure appeared beside the attackers, gesturing wildly. With the water and Mark's near-sightedness blurring its form, it looked like a praying mantis. The Chessmen pulled their victim back and dropped him on the tile.

Mark sat up, gasping and coughing. Water streamed out of his hair and into his eyes. He was almost as surprised as he was relieved. He certainly hadn't expected *Greg* to save him.

The sophomore crouched beside him. "Are you okay?"

"I guess," Mark wheezed.

"I'm sorry that happened. It was so stupid." Greg turned to the other cadets. "How could we have a spy?" he demanded scornfully. "If we did, he would have told somebody where and when to nail us Sunday night."

"Maybe I made a mistake," Warren said grudgingly.

"Maybe you did." Greg turned back to Mark. "You see why I want *you* in the Chessmen? *You've* got some brain cells wired together. Please, help me get these Cooper creeps off our backs. I promise it'll be fun, just like before." His dark eyes gazed into Mark's. Up close, they looked like wet, black stones.

Mark's dislike of Barry and his friends started trickling back. Maybe he *should* help the Chessmen harass them, if only to repay Greg for saving his life.

No! He tore his eyes away from Greg's and slammed his fist down on the floor. The jolt of pain cleared his head. "Forget it," he said.

Greg sighed. "All right. We can find out who Barry's friends are by watching him, so I guess we can manage without you if we have to."

"What if he tells somebody about us *now?*" Warren asked. Other cadets murmured. For a second, Mark was afraid they'd jump him again.

"I won't," he said. "I swear. After all, you're my friends." One of the Chessmen spat. Others stared coldly.

"Fair enough," Greg said. "Now take off. The rest of us have things to talk about."

Mark waded into the pool, retrieved his glasses, then walked to the door, his wet pant legs slapping. As he pulled it open, Warren said, "I still say—"

"Relax," Greg replied. "Everything's under control."

Nine

Sitting alone in the cafeteria—or mess, as they called it in Hudson talk—Mark picked up one of his cooling french fries. He stared at it, then dropped it back on his plate, finally admitting that he wasn't hungry. He knew that he had stopped for lunch just to stall. He rose, carried his tray to the dishwashers' window, then trudged, shoulders hunched, toward Colonel Green's office. His footsteps echoed down the long, gloomy corridors.

He didn't *want* to rat on the Chessmen. He'd never squealed on anyone in his life. But the "secret brotherhood" had moved way beyond practical jokes. Last night, they'd nearly killed him, so how long could it be before they hurt somebody else? For everyone's sake, including their own, they had to be stopped.

As he neared his destination, he nervously tightened and straightened his black tie. He made sure his gray coat was properly buttoned, and the navy-blue braid on his left shoulder hung correctly. Colonel Green hated a sloppy uniform, and Mark wanted to make a good impression.

Sergeant Saunders, Colonel Green's assistant, stepped out of an intersecting hall. He was a burly man in his fifties, his skin brown and cracked from a lifetime in the sun. When he spotted Mark, his pale blue, droopy-lidded eyes narrowed. "So there you are," he said.

Mark wondered what he meant. "I need to see the colonel," he said.

"What a coincidence," Sergeant Saunders said. "He wants to see you, too. Come on." He ushered Mark down the corridor, through his own office, and into the headmaster's.

The room held the sweetish tang of pipe tobacco. On the walls hung crossed sabers and rifles, and on top of Colonel Green's wide desk a gilded hand grenade sat weighting a stack of loose papers. The colonel sat scowling in his swivel chair. To Mark's surprise, a young policeman with dark, curly hair and a trimmed mustache occupied the green leather couch, a cardboard box beside his feet.

"When I found him, he said *he* wanted to talk to *you*," Sergeant Saunders said.

"Good," Colonel Green replied. He looked Mark up and down, then waved at the chair beside the desk. "Sit down, cadet. This is Officer Murphy, from the Cooper Hollow Police. He's looking into the recent vandalism. I assume that's what's on your mind, too."

"Yes, sir," Mark said, feeling confused. "I can tell you everything about it. But how did you know to ask me?"

"First, say what you want to say," Officer Murphy said. "We'll answer your questions afterward."

So Mark told them everything except for his half-baked fancies about the Chessmen's bodies changing, and Greg being able to control people's minds. He didn't want to sound crazy.

When he finished, the colonel and Officer Murphy exchanged glances. "That's . . . an interesting story," the policeman said.

46

"You sound like you don't believe it," Mark said. "I admitted that I helped break the trophies and tear down the bleachers. Why would I do that if I was lying?"

Officer Murphy scratched his jaw. "You confessed to *some* wrongdoing, but you told us somebody else was the instigator, and you denied having anything to do with killing the goat. Here's what I'm thinking. A boy breaks the law. Then someone in authority comes looking for him. The boy figures he's more or less busted, he can't talk himself all the way out of hot water, but maybe he'll get part way out if he can shift some of the blame onto other kids. So he makes up a story on the spot."

Mark's mouth was dry. He had to swallow before he could speak. "But it's *not* just a story. Why do you think it is?"

Colonel Green said, "Several cadets spoke to me this morning. They all said you boasted that you were solely responsible for the destruction at Cooper High and here too."

Mark shook his head. "No! It was Greg and the others who came to you, wasn't it? *They're* lying! Framing me! They were afraid I was going to tell on them, so they decided to fix it so you wouldn't believe me!"

"They also said that you'd shown them souvenirs you'd taken Sunday night," Officer Murphy said. "So Colonel Green searched your room. He found these in your footlocker." He reached into the cardboard box. Brought out severed horns, hooves, and ears in neatly labeled plastic bags.

Mark felt himself start to tremble. He tried to stop. Tried to think. "The Chessmen planted those things. Look, can't you see, their story doesn't make sense. I couldn't do all that damage by myself."

Packing away the evidence, Officer Murphy said, "If you stole a truck, and used it to push or pull things over, maybe you could. Anyway, here's the bottom line. The goat parts were in your trunk. It's nine kids' word against yours. It makes more sense that one new kid is having problems than several boys, some of whom we've known for years, have all turned into troublemakers at once. So I have to place you under arrest." He unbuttoned the flap on his breast pocket, took out a laminated card, and started reading Mark his *Miranda* rights.

For a moment, the boy was lightheaded with panic. Then a steely determination spread through him. It couldn't quell his fear, but it blunted it.

Since he was still the only one who had any idea what was really happening, he was also the only hope of stopping people from getting hurt. He couldn't do anything from jail, so he wasn't going.

Officer Murphy finished reading the card. Trying to make his voice as meek and childlike as possible, Mark said, "I'm glad you caught me. I didn't *want* to kill the goat. I didn't want to do any of it. But I hear these voices, and they said they'd hurt me if I didn't."

The policeman nodded. "I understand. Don't worry, we won't let anything hurt you anymore."

Mark blinked as if he was struggling not to cry. "Am I going to prison?"

"No," Officer Murphy said. "First, you'll be in the juvenile detention center. It's okay there, honest. After your hearing, the court will send you to a treatment program. Nobody's out to punish you. We just want to help you solve your problems."

Mark said, "Thank you. I need help. I feel so bad."

Colonel Green cleared his throat. "I'll contact the boy's parents. They're in some tiny village in South

America, so don't expect to hear from them right away."

"Okay," the curly-headed policeman said. He looked at Mark. "We should get going." He reached for the gleaming handcuffs on his belt.

The cadet swallowed. He was about to find out if his pathetic act had paid off. "Please," he said, "don't make me wear those. They look like they hurt, and I don't want my friends to see me in them."

The officer studied him. The teenager held his breath. Finally the cop said, "Okay. I'm trusting you to behave."

As they walked toward the building's main entrance, Mark wracked his brain, trying to come up with an escape plan. He'd kept his hands free, but that wouldn't mean a thing once Officer Murphy locked him in the back of his prowl car. He had to break away *now*, and for that he needed a distraction.

Finally, he got an idea. He stumbled, doubled over, and clutched his stomach. "What is it?" Officer Murphy asked.

"My gut hurts," Mark whined. "I need to go to the bathroom *bad*."

"Okay," the policeman said, looking around. "There's one right over—"

Mark stamped on the cop's foot, kicked him in the shin, and shoved him. He reeled, bumped into a drinking fountain, and fell. The cardboard box flew out from under his arm, scattering its grisly contents across the floor.

Mark ran.

Ten

After a moment, Mark heard Officer Murphy's footsteps pounding after him. He tried to run faster.

The bell trilled. Doors opened and chattering cadets surged out. Mark almost ran into a short, frizzy-haired guy. He shoved him out of the way, and the boy squawked in outrage.

"Stop that kid!" Officer Murphy yelled.

Mark burst out of the hall into the domed atrium, scrambled across it toward the exit. His feet slipped on the gleaming marble floor. Faces gaped from the balconies above.

When he ran out onto the portico, he saw that Officer Murphy's squad car was parked near the toppled statue. He bounded down the stairs and stooped to peer through the vehicle's window. The key wasn't in the ignition, so he dashed on across the lawn.

When he glanced back, Officer Murphy was tearing down the steps. He unlocked the squad car and jumped in.

Mark's foot caught on something. He fell, and pain stabbed through his elbow. He rolled to his feet and ran on.

At his back, an engine roared. Then a siren wailed, the keening growing louder. He veered, weaving through shrubs and trees, so Officer Murphy couldn't drive straight at him.

He reached the wall forty feet ahead of his pursuer. He leaped, grabbed the top, swung himself over, and ran on down a path into the woods.

When the academy disappeared from view, he left the trail. He stumbled to a stop behind a stand of brush, flopped down, and slumped there panting.

After a minute, he heard footsteps. His pulse sped up again. He could feel it beating in his neck.

"Mark," Officer Murphy called, his voice amplified and distorted by a bullhorn. "Please, come out. I swear, we only want to help you."

Mark rose and tiptoed away from the sound.

"Think about it," Officer Murphy pleaded. "I radioed for help. There are a lot of people looking for you. You can't get away. But suppose you could. What would you do then? You can't stay in the woods forever."

The cadet skulked on. Fallen leaves crunched beneath his feet.

He froze, but it was too late. He could already hear Officer Murphy tramping in his direction. A radio squawked and crackled.

Mark ran, hurtling down one slope and laboring up another. When he reached the top, there was a slim, dark-haired policewoman fifty feet in front of him. She said, "Okay, kid, stay right there," and strode toward him.

Mark pivoted and dashed to his right. The woman cursed and pounded after him.

Before long the cadet lost track of what direction he was traveling. Every breath stabbed pain through his chest, and his legs were going numb. He began to fear that Officer Murphy was right: he couldn't possibly get away.

He stumbled to the top of another hill and saw the grimy brick walls of the Nightmare Club through the trees ahead. He wondered if he could hide inside the building.

Only if his pursuers didn't see him enter, he reasoned. He had to increase his lead enough to get out of their sight. He strained to make his weary legs run faster.

He crashed through brush, raced between trees. Twigs scratched him. Alternately revealed and concealed by the foliage, the Nightmare Club appeared and vanished like a mirage.

Finally he tore through a thicket into its backyard. Gasping, praying that the back door was unlocked, he staggered across the narrow strip of grass.

He twisted the knob. The door swung open. He lurched through and locked it behind him.

Looking around, he found himself in a hallway. Light and a rumbling sound spilled from an opening in the righthand wall. Beyond that was a staircase.

The light and noise made Mark afraid to stay where he was. Maybe the best way to avoid being caught trespassing would be to hide upstairs. It was a big building, and Jenny and her dad were only two people. There were probably rooms on the second floor they never used.

He crept to the gap in the wall and peeked inside. He was looking into the Nightmare Club's kitchen. Her back turned, Jenny stood at a counter slicing pepperoni. Her long knife gleamed in the fluorescent light. The rumbling he had heard sounded from the dishwasher.

Holding his breath, Mark tried to tiptoe by. Fatigue made him sway, and his shoulder brushed a picture off the wall. It banged on the floor.

Mark cringed. Surely even with the dishwasher running, Jenny must have heard the crash. But she didn't turn around.

Trembling, Mark sneaked up the stairs. As he reached the landing, the dishwasher switched off. A second later, someone knocked on the back door.

Jenny's footsteps pattered down the hall. The door clicked. "Sam! Good to see you," the blond woman said.

"Hi, Jen," Officer Murphy wheezed. Mark was pleased that the cop sounded as winded as he was. "We're looking for a juvenile. A cadet. Officer Montoya and I were trying to herd him toward some guys who were waiting to grab him, but he disappeared. It occurred to me that he might have slipped in here."

"You're the first living soul I've seen all day," Jenny answered. "And I've been in the kitchen since early this morning."

"Then I'd better start beating the bushes again," the policeman said wearily. "If you do see the kid, don't approach him. He's got problems. He chopped up Cooper High's pet goat, and for all I know, he could do the same to a person."

"I'll be careful," Jenny said. "You do the same." The door clicked shut.

Mark discovered he was holding his breath. He let it out, then crept up, wincing every time a floorboard creaked. Below, Jenny started humming a waltz.

All the doors on the second floor were closed. Mark skulked to the one farthest from the stairs and warily cracked it open. The room inside had no furniture, though scars on the floor showed where some had been. Cobwebs curtained the window, and dust floated in the air.

Mark stepped inside, shut the door, and sat down with his back against the wall. Okay, what's the plan? he asked himself. I ran away to stop the Chessmen, so how am I going to do it?

He couldn't imagine. He was too scared and tired to think. Hoping a moment's rest would clear his head, he closed his eyes.

Eleven

When Mark opened his eyes, he was lying on a cot. Seven other boys, a couple about his age, the rest younger, lay on similar beds around him. One was snoring. A shaft of silver moonlight shone through the window.

Mark threw off his covers and sat up. He was wearing a white nightshirt. He peered about, hunting his glasses, and found a pair on the stand beside his cot. They weren't his, the frames were wire, not plastic, but when he tried them on, he discovered that the lenses had been ground to his prescription.

Something prompted him to go to the window.

Beyond the pane, trees writhed. Dry leaves whirled from the branches.

Except for the motion of the trees, there didn't seem to be anything to see. He opened the window and leaned out for a better view. The moaning wind toyed with his hair.

When he looked to the left, he saw that the outside of the Nightmare Club had changed like everything else. Someone had added a wing made of wood to the original structure, as if there'd been a crying need for more space. Shadowy figures skulked around it. It was hard to be sure in the darkness, but Mark thought that some were subtly deformed.

55

Hammering clattered. Liquid splashed, and the smell of kerosene filled the air. Matches flared. "Don't!" Mark screamed.

Sections of the annex wall exploded into flame. Mark flinched at the sudden glare and blast of heat. The blaze revealed that the arsonists were clad in gray uniforms with navy trim, not quite identical to the one Mark had been wearing, but unmistakably Hudson outfits anyway.

A tall, thin cadet looked up at the window and grinned. It was Greg Tobias, one eye clear and the other bloodshot, a snowfall of white hair on his left epaulet.

Crackling sheets of flame ran up the wooden wall. The cadets hooted and danced.

Mark whirled to face the sleepers. "Get up!" he yelled, but they didn't stir. He grabbed one by the shoulders and shook him. The boy's head flopped back and forth. He groaned, but still didn't wake.

Mark dropped him and ran to the next room. He couldn't rouse the kids in that one either. He dashed on, threw open doors till he found an adult, a man with a gray handlebar mustache sprawled on his back in his bed. Mark shrieked at him, pounded his chest, then pinched his cheek as hard as he could. The man mumbled and squirmed, but his eyes wouldn't open.

The cadet ran down to the ground floor. The teen club was gone. In its place he found a dining room filled with long tables, and gaslit parlors furnished with ratty sofas and ticking clocks. He wasted a precious minute blundering around before he located the door to the annex.

The brass knob was burning hot. Gritting his teeth, he gripped and turned it. The door wouldn't open. For an instant, he assumed it was locked, then noticed the nails that pinned it to the frame.

56

A cadet with a hammer stepped out of the shadows. His eyes shone amber in the gloom. "We nailed all the doors," he said. "The shutters, too. Even if people wake up in the next few minutes, everyone in the addition is going to burn."

Mark said, "Give me the hammer." If he had it, he could break the door down, or pull the nails out.

The cadet grinned, exposing teeth grown long and jagged. "Sure, take it." Swinging the tool over his head, he sprang.

Mark lunged to meet him, and punched him in the mouth. Teeth broke against his knuckles, cutting them. He tried to grapple his attacker.

The arsonist shoved him. Mark reeled backward, tripped over a low table, and crashed to the floor.

His attacker dove on top of him, driving the breath out of his lungs. The hammer flashed at his forehead . . .

. . . and he awoke sitting alone on a hard floor. He was wearing his own glasses and sweaty uniform, and his right hand wasn't blistered or gashed anymore.

It was just a dream, he thought shakily. He lifted his head, gasped, and recoiled, pressing his body against the wall.

A figure like a statue made of black sticks loomed over him. He thought it had once been a boy, though its body was too charred to be sure. It smelled like roasting meat.

After a while, it faded, as though the sunlight pouring through the grimy, cobwebbed window was making it burn again. Its stink lingered a little longer, but soon, that too was gone.

Mark felt his heart pounding, heard himself panting. Taking deep breaths, he tried to calm down, and to make sense of what had happened.

Eventually he decided that the Nightmare Club really was haunted, and he'd just met one of its phantoms. He'd never believed in such things, but what other explanation was there? And the ghost had made him dream about the orphanage fire.

If it had been a *true* dream—and he couldn't think of any reason for the ghost to show him a false one—then all his fears, even the ones that had seemed ridiculous, were justified. There *was* something unnatural about Greg Tobias. He *did* have superhuman powers. A hundred years ago he'd used them to make some cadets commit mass murder, and he was probably getting the Chessmen ready to do the same thing.

And I'm the only one who knows, Mark thought, trembling. But I don't know what to do about it! I didn't know even when I thought Greg was just a regular kid! He struggled to come up with a strategy. He wasn't sure of the whole plan, but eventually he realized what his next move had to be.

Later that afternoon, he prowled through the Nightmare Club's upper floor until he found an office. Musty-smelling books crammed the wall shelves and sat in stacks on the floor. On a marble stand by a rolltop desk was a black rotary phone.

Mark slipped into the room, closed the door, and picked up the receiver. For a moment, he couldn't remember the number he wanted, but then it popped into his head.

As he dialed, he thought, please, be there. And please, be the one who answers.

The phone rang four times. "Hello," Laurie said.

Mark swallowed. "It's Mark. Can you talk?"

"I—I guess," she faltered, her voice softer. "Hold on." Her phone clunked down on a hard surface. A door clicked shut. "Okay, I'm back."

"I had some trouble today."

"I heard. People say the police found out you killed

our mascot."

"I swear, I didn't. The cadets who did framed me because they were afraid I was going to squeal on them."

"If you're innocent, you have to turn yourself in. It's the only way to straighten things out. In fact, even if you're guilty —"

"You don't understand," he said. "Something awful's happening, something I could never make the cops believe. I have to stay free to stop it, and I need you to help me. My folks are in South America and everyone at Hudson's turned against me, so you're the only person I can ask."

For a moment, she didn't answer. He would have bet money that he knew what she was thinking, pretty much the same thing Officer Murphy had told Jenny: if he *had* killed the goat, he might do the same to her. "What do you think is happening?" she asked at last.

"I can't explain now. It's going to take time, and if somebody picks up another extension and hears me talking, he could tell the police where I am. But it involves Barry. He's in danger."

"Look, you can't expect —"

"*Please,*" Mark said. "We talked a lot Saturday night. You know me now. Do you really think I'm crazy? Or sick enough to kill a helpless animal for fun?"

"No," Laurie said. "So what do you want me to do?"

Twelve

Crouched behind a sharp-smelling pine tree, Mark peeked through its branches. Footsteps padded, then a striding figure rounded the bend in the path. The cadet pulled two boughs apart for a better view, then scowled in disappointment. The walker was a guy.

Mark had slipped out of the Nightmare Club around sunset, late enough for the cops to have given up their search, but early enough to avoid kids on their way to the teen cafe. It hadn't taken him long to find a hiding place overlooking the trail. When Laurie showed up, he'd hail her.

If she showed up. Maybe her parents had made her stay home. Or maybe she'd decided she was afraid to come.

He told himself to think positive. And at that instant, she came into view, a white shopping bag swinging in her hand. She wore a knit cap on her head, and the collar of her jacket was turned up against the breeze. She kept glancing from side to side.

He rose and stepped from behind the pine. "Over here!" he called.

She jumped. "Jeez! You just about gave me a heart attack."

"Sorry. Come here." She hesitated. "Or I can come down there. I just thought it was a bad idea to talk on the trail. Somebody else could come along."

"You're right. I'll come to you." She climbed toward him. He led her over a rise, out of sight of the path.

Now that she was here, Mark felt nervous. How could he explain the crazy things that had happened? "Thanks for meeting me," he said. "I, uh, guess you bought the stuff."

"Yeah. It took nearly every penny I had, too." She handed him the bag.

As he opened it, he smelled hot, greasy meat. For an instant, it reminded him of the fire victim's ghost, and he was afraid it was going to make him sick. Then his mouth watered, his stomach growled, and he realized he was starving. He grabbed the fast-food burger, tore the wrapper off, and wolfed it down.

"You didn't say anything about supper, but I figured you might want some," Laurie said. His mouth full, he nodded his thanks.

The clothes in the sack were black: an Iron Maiden tee-shirt with a leering zombie on it; faded, tattered jeans; sneakers; socks; a studded leather belt with a skull on the buckle; and matching wrist bands. There was also an ear clip with a miniature axe dangling at the end of a half-inch chain.

"I've never worn this kind of stuff," said Mark. "My mom would have gone bonkers."

"Good," Laurie said, "since we're trying to disguise you. The cops are looking for a Hudson guy, and I figured that a headbanger looks about as little like a cadet as anyone can. Try it on."

He went behind a pine. It was a relief to peel off his sweat-stained uniform. The night air chilled his skin. When he'd changed, he stepped from behind the tree. "How do I look?" he asked.

Her head cocked, she studied him. "Not that great. But different, and that's what's important. The glasses aren't right. Can you do without them?"

"Most times."

"Well, when you can, put them in your pocket. The hair's wrong, too. Maybe later we can at least change the color, mousse it, get it spiky." She looked him in the eye. "Okay, Mark, I did what you wanted. If anybody finds out, I could be arrested for helping a fugitive. Now tell me what the heck is going on."

He still hadn't thought of a way to make it sound convincing. He took a deep breath, and blundered through the whole story as best he could, certain every moment that he sounded psycho.

She listened to the whole thing without interrupting. When he finished, she said, "I can't believe you wrecked my school's trophies, didn't tell me, and then started dating me. That's so dishonest. It's like you didn't respect me at all."

"I know," Mark said, surprised that out of everything he'd said, she'd chosen that to remark on. "I'm sorry."

She sighed. "I'll give you the benefit of the doubt. Maybe you would have acted different if Greg hadn't put his spell on you. But don't you lie to me again."

He blinked. "Does this mean you believe me? The whole thing?"

Laurie nodded. "Dumb as it sounds, I guess I do. See, you came to the right girl. I've read books about witchcraft, UFOs, and astrology. I've always kind of believed all the old Hollow spook stories, even though I've never seen a ghost myself. And what's happening between Cooper High and Hudson is so weird that maybe a hundred year-old monster *is* the only explanation. There's always been a feud, but this year, things have gone completely nuts."

For a moment, Mark thought he was going to cry. Until that instant, he hadn't realized how alone he felt and how badly he needed someone to share the secret.

"Do you think we could convince anyone else?" he asked.

"Without proof? Not a chance. Until we get some, we're going to have to deal with this ourselves. Have you made a plan?"

"Not really."

She grimaced. "Terrific."

"Hey, I've been busy. Shaking off Greg's hypnotism. Running from cops. Getting haunted. It cuts into your time."

"Okay," she said. "Let's think about what we can do. *How* did you break Greg's control?"

"I guess I'm just resistant. Who knows, maybe moving all the time, always being the outsider, has made me independent. Anyway, once I got rid of my chess piece, I didn't have a lot of trouble."

"What if we got rid of all the pieces?"

"I don't know how you'd do that. Besides, the pieces just magnify the control. They don't create it."

"Well, then . . ." She hesitated. "Darn it, we know a little, but not enough to give us an idea."

"Maybe we can find out more," he said. "There must have been newspaper stories about the fire. You could read them."

"Yeah," she said, "I bet they're in the library. I'll look tomorrow afternoon, then meet you here after dark. What'll you do, hide in the club till then?"

"If I can sneak back in. Otherwise, I'll stay in the woods. I don't want to go into town until I have to. Even dressed like this, I might get recognized, or hassled for being out of school."

"In that case, I'll bring more food." She glanced at

63

her watch. "Crap! It's late. I've got to get home, or my dad won't let me out tomorrow."

"Please, stay one more minute. There's something else I've got to say. Are you sure you want to keep helping me? I know I asked you, and I need you, but maybe you shouldn't. This could get as dangerous for you as it's been for me."

"I know — I'm not stupid. It could get nasty. But I'm not going to stand aside and let Barry get hurt, or you either. Look, don't worry, somehow we'll make things come out okay." She kissed him, then headed toward the path. In a moment, she'd vanished into the night.

Thirteen

Mark wished he owned a watch. He felt as if he'd been waiting for hours. Last night, he'd been worried that Laurie wouldn't come. Now he was afraid she *couldn't*. What if Greg had somehow sensed that she was working against him, and had done something to stop her?

At last a figure scurried down the trail. When it stepped into a patch of moonlight, Mark released his breath. It was Laurie. He jumped up and called her name.

She hurried up the slope, slipping on fallen leaves, a white paper bag in her hand. He ran down and met her halfway.

Smiling, she said, "We've got to stop meeting like this." Then she frowned. "Hey, are you okay? You look like you've seen a ghost. I mean, another ghost."

"I'm all right. I was just getting worried about you."

"Really? It's not late. Though I guess if I'd been the one waiting in the dark, it would seem that way to me." She handed him the bag. He opened it and found a roast-beef sandwich and french fries. "Did you get back in the Nightmare Club last night?"

"Yeah," he replied, grabbing some fries. "Makes

you wonder if those people ever lock their doors." They hiked toward the top of the slope. "What's going on in the Hollow?"

"Nothing good. One of Barry's friends got beaten up bad enough to go to the hospital. He said he never got a good look at the guys who jumped him. I bet that's because he thinks he and his buddies should settle the score themselves."

"Which will make the Chessmen want to get even," Mark said grimly, "until eventually, people start getting killed. What did you find out at the library?"

"Quite a bit," Laurie said. "For one thing, the orphanage fire happened one hundred years ago *exactly.*"

Mark frowned. "What do you think that means?"

Laurie shrugged. "Beats me, but it seems like it ought to mean *something.* Anyway, the orphans and cadets never liked one another, and during the weeks leading up to the fire, things really got out of control. There were cruel practical jokes, and fights almost every day. Kids got seriously injured."

"And now history's repeating itself."

"Tell me about it."

"Did any of the stories mention Greg Tobias?"

"Not that time around. But in the *1790s* —"

"The what?"

Laurie grinned, obviously pleased with herself. "I figured that if Greg was in the Hollow exactly one hundred years ago, he might have been around a century before that. There was no newspaper here during that time, but people have written history books about it."

"And they talked about Greg?"

"I think so. Back then, the settlers and the local Indians were living in peace. Until a young man named Toby Gregson convinced some whites that the tribe was turning hostile. The guys who believed him started harassing the Indians, and of course, some of the braves struck back. To make a long story short, a mob wound up massacreing most of the Indian village. Afterward, when Toby disappeared, some people claimed he'd been a warlock, and served an evil spirit that lived in the forest."

Mark grimaced. "Do you believe in that kind of junk?"

Laurie shrugged. "Don't we already believe in ghosts? Maybe there is a guy who's lived hundreds of years and has *some* kind of power that turns ordinary people into deformed killers. Why not?"

"Why not." Mark echoed. He ate more fries. They were getting cold, and needed salt, but since he hadn't eaten for twenty-four hours, they tasted good anyway. "Did you find out anything else?"

"No. What did you expect? I thought I did good, getting this much."

"You did great," he said. "I never would have thought to check out the 1700s. But we still have too many unanswered questions. *Why* does Greg do this every hundred years? Is it just his idea of fun, or is there more to it? Why did I see his face get all pruny? And if he's a cold-blooded killer, why didn't he let the Chessmen drown me? They probably could have made it look like an accident."

She nodded thoughtfully. "You're right. And you know what the biggest question is? Aside from what we're going to do about all this, of course."

"What?"

"We know what's making the Chessmen crazy. But guys from my school are acting just as weird. What's messing with *their* heads?"

"Maybe Greg is influencing them, too."

"I don't think so," Laurie said. "If he can do it from

far away, without talking to his victims, then why didn't he control the cadets that way? Why did he bother to enroll at Hudson?"

"To get a good seat for the fight?"

"I don't think so. I think there's a whole other side to this, something we haven't got a handle on at all."

Mark smiled crookedly. "Great. Like it wasn't confusing enough already."

"Look on the bright side. We don't know how to break Greg's hold over the Chessmen. But maybe if we learn what's driving the Cooper guys nuts, we can stop that. And if we get *either* side to stop provoking the other, we break the cycle that leads to the violence. Fortunately, my brother is one of the Cooper psychos. It shouldn't be too hard for me to snoop into his business. I'll meet you here tomorrow—"

"Forget that," Mark said. "I'm snooping with you."

Laurie shook her head. "Bad idea. Like you said, if you go into town, somebody might recognize you."

"Yeah, but if Barry catches you spying, he might hurt you to protect his secrets. I know you hate to think that, but take it from somebody else who was hypnotized, he's not the same person anymore. So I won't let you poke around alone."

"I think you're just tired of being stuck in the woods," she said. "But all right, we'll do it your way. I've got to admit, I'll feel better if somebody's watching my back."

Fourteen

Mark squinted, trying to make sense of the fuzzy shapes floating in the dark. The streetlights and the illuminated windows of the houses were smears of glow.

Laurie's hand squeezed his. "Stop screwing up your face," she said. "You look like a mole. I thought you said you could see without your glasses."

"I can, enough to get by, most of the time. But I *hate* not being able to see things far away. Especially now that people are out to get me."

Her fingers gently tightened again. "I don't blame you. Do you think we'll find anything?"

"I don't know, but I guess we should look. Detectives in stories always go through people's stuff."

They walked on down the maple-lined street. The spicy aroma of a barbecue wafted from one house, and a sitcom's laugh track blared from another. Mark wondered when he'd be able to veg in front of a TV again. The thought made him feel sad.

"There's my house," Laurie said. "Wait here while I check things out." She hurried down the sidewalk, then skulked into her yard.

Mark leaned against somebody's picket fence, trying to look as if he belonged there. A car turned a corner and came toward him. Its headlights dazed him. It was almost on top of him before he made out the crash lights on its roof.

His mouth went dry. He didn't know what to do. If the policeman had recognized him, he'd better run. But if the cop didn't know who he was, he didn't want to arouse his suspicions by fleeing. Finally he decided to stay where he was.

The prowl car stopped beside him. The window rolled down.

Mark trembled. Almost bolted. Then it occurred to him that if the cop had identified him, he probably would have turned on his emergency lights and siren and jumped out to arrest him. So maybe the man *didn't* know him. After all, it was dark, he was more or less in disguise, and the car was in the street, several feet from the fence. So he held himself in place.

"Do you live around here?" the policeman asked.

"No, sir," Mark answered, "but this is my friend's house. He'll be out in a minute."

The policeman said, "I'll be back this way in less than half an hour. I don't want to see you hanging around when I get back." He rolled up his window and drove on. Mark slumped with relief.

A minute later, Laurie trotted back. "Mom and Dad are watching TV," she said. "Barry's gone off somewhere as usual. We'll go in the back way."

"Sounds like a plan to me," Mark said. "I'm getting good at sneaking in back doors."

Laurie led him around the side of her white wooden house. Rose bushes, their flowers black in the gloom, grew at the base of the wall. Their scent was almost too sweet, as if their blooms were rotting.

As the teenagers stepped into the backyard, luminous eyes blazed. An inhuman voice yowled. Mark jumped.

Laurie said, "Chill, Vladimir, it's me." The gray cat padded up and rubbed against her legs.

She stooped to scratch its head, then cracked the door open and peeked through. "The coast is still clear," she whispered.

They crept through a dark kitchen, then up a flight of stairs. The voices of Sam and Norm from a *Cheers* rerun murmured after them.

When they reached the upper floor, Laurie ushered him through the first door on the right, closed it, and flipped on the light. Blinking, he peered around.

Barry's room was a typical guy's bedroom. Dirty socks littered the floor. A chemistry text and a doodle-covered spiral notebook lay on the unmade bed. A stereo and rows of CDs occupied the shelves above the desk, and posters of rock bands and barely-dressed women decorated the walls.

"Let's hurry," said Laurie, pulling open the top dresser drawer. Mark put on his glasses, paused for an instant to enjoy the sudden clarity of vision, then started flipping through the notebook.

It was Barry's class notes. But he'd filled the margins with Traci Elmore's name, and pictures of cadets with knives sticking out of their eyes, throats, and hearts. Mark shivered.

"This might be something," Laurie said. She held out what looked like a pair of brass rods fastened together. It still had a price sticker clinging to it. "But I don't know what."

Mark took the device and opened it, exposing a long, double-edged blade. "It's a butterfly knife," he said.

"Jeez! That thing could really hurt somebody."

"And I think Barry knows that." He showed her the notebook.

71

"Crap! He's worse off than I thought!" She returned to the drawer, pawed through stacks of folded tee-shirts. "Here're two cans of spray paint, one red and one white. And look at this!" She held up a wooden carving of a horse's head.

"A chess knight," Mark said. "Only his is red instead of gray, like mine was."

"I'm going to burn it," Laurie said.

"No."

"Yes. I can't let Barry cut people up."

"But you don't know that destroying the knight will stop him. The person controlling him might give him a replacement. Worse, he might figure out you're the one who stole the first one. You can't risk that. We shouldn't make that kind of move until we're ready to solve the whole problem."

"That's easy for you to say. You—" She pivoted. "Did you hear that?"

"No," he said, but then he did. People were clumping up the stairs.

"One of those guys is Barry," Laurie whispered. "I know his footsteps. One of us should have watched for him out the window!"

"Turn off the light and hide."

"Too late. They probably already saw it. I'll talk, you hide."

He fumbled the knife shut, handed it to her, tossed the notebook down, and scrambled under the bed. He heard her hurriedly stowing the weapon, paint, and chess piece away.

The drawer bumped shut. A second later, the door swung open. From beneath the bed, Mark could only see two pairs of feet. "Hi," Laurie said.

"What are you doing?" Barry asked.

"Looking for all the CDs you've borrowed," Laurie answered. "I hardly have anything left to listen to."

"You shouldn't be in here. I don't go in your stuff without asking."

"Then how did you get all my music?" Laurie demanded. A moment passed and Mark heard plastic clattering. Next, two CD cases fell on the rug and were picked up. Finally, Laurie's feet marched out and the door slammed behind her.

Immediately a dresser drawer slid open. "It's okay," Barry said. "Everything's still here."

"Is it just like you left it?" his companion asked. Mark recognized the voice; it was the kid who'd wanted to help Barry beat him up.

"Uh-huh."

"She still could have been snooping—"

"Laurie wouldn't spy on me," Barry said. "She's bossy and she makes me crazy, but she's a good kid. That's why I'm going to make sure nobody hurts her. I'm ready. Let's go." The drawer bumped shut. The two boys strode out the door and down the stairs.

After a few silent minutes, Laurie reentered the room. Mark crawled from under the bed, rose, and brushed the dust off his shirt. "Are they gone?"

"Yeah. Down the street." She opened the drawer and rummaged through it. "Crap! He took everything, including the knife!"

Mark said, "We'd better follow them."

Fifteen

"I wish you'd take off the glasses," Laurie whispered. "They make you look too much like you."

"If Barry or his friend start to look back, I need to *see* so I can duck behind cover," Mark replied.

"I guess," the girl said dubiously. Half a block ahead, the two Cooper High guys — or Red Chessmen, as Mark had begun to think of them — disappeared around a corner.

"Darn," Laurie said. She walked faster.

The cadet took hold of her forearm. "Take it easy."

"They could get away."

"If they do, they do. If we get too close and they spot us, we won't learn anything anyway, besides which, they're liable to come after us. Nobody's chased me or tried to hurt me in almost two days. I want to see how long I can keep that going."

She sighed. "I guess you're right."

They crept on down the sidewalk, past a hydrant and an overturned tricycle. Mark heard the wind rustle the dry leaves, just like it had in his dream. He fought to keep his nerves steady.

"Can I ask you something, Mark?" asked Laurie.

"Sure."

"You said I might not want to get involved in this mess. But don't *you* want to walk away from it? You're

74

risking your neck to save guys you've only known a few weeks."

"Yeah," he said, "but one of them is *your* brother. Besides, when I got to the Hollow, I felt lonely, like I have most of my life. Then, all of a sudden, I had friends. But just when I was getting used to it, the same power that gave them to me turned them against me. That really makes me mad. I want to get even."

She smiled at him. "Cheer up, you've still got one pal. I like you fine. I mean, for a rich-brat cadet."

He felt himself blush. He hoped she couldn't see it. "Thanks. I like you, too, even if you are bossy."

"What?"

"That's what I heard Barry tell his friend."

"That creep! After we fix his brain, I'm going to kill him and his pal Roger, too."

As they approached the corner, Mark was suddenly sure that the Red Chessmen were lying in wait around the corner. He held up his hand, signaling Laurie to stop, then tiptoed forward until he could see down the side street.

An instant later, he grimaced at his cowardice, not that he really blamed himself for feeling edgy. Barry and Roger were still well ahead of him. They turned again, heading up a driveway.

"It's okay," Mark said. Laurie hurried to his side. He pointed. "They went to that house. The one with the MG parked in front."

"Jim and Jerry Thomas, two of Barry's other friends, live there."

Laurie and Mark slunk down the side street, then up the driveway, keeping in the shadow of the hedge that grew beside it. A drone of conversation drew them toward the rear of the house.

Despite the evening chill, Barry, Roger, and several other guys—because of the dark, Mark couldn't tell

75

exactly how many—were lounging on a screened-in patio. Chips crunched as a bag passed from hand to hand. The two spies crept closer, then crouched behind a tall bush at the corner of the enclosure.

At first, the Cooper High boys talked about the destruction of their trophies and bleachers, the killing of their mascot, and the attack on their friend. Somehow, they understood that a group of cadets, not just Mark, was responsible for the ongoing harassment, though they still considered him one of the gang. They even knew some of the other Gray Chessmen's names.

After a while, the discussion turned to an older outrage, Wes Lombard's supposed murder of Traci Elmore. As Mark listened, the hairs on the nape of his neck stood on end. Because the Red Chessmen weren't just speculating about the killing. Voices trembling, they were describing it, one knife cut at a time, as if they'd seen it happen. Or as if they were watching it that instant.

And gradually, Mark began to see it himself. A once-lovely girl lay on the ground, thrashing and begging for mercy. Her face was wet with tears. Blood soaked her white Cooper High cheerleader's sweater. A cadet laughed and taunted, as he slashed and stabbed. The coppery stench of gore filled the air.

Then suddenly Mark's perspective shifted. Now *he* was the victim, struggling futilely to break free. The knife stung him over and over again. He felt himself weakening.

Finally, Traci shuddered. Her throat rattled, and she stopped squirming. As she died, the dream ended.

A hand gripped his real-life shoulder and shook him. The vision dissolved. He realized he must have looked so shaken that Laurie was afraid he was going to cry out.

For a while, the Red Chessmen sat silently. Then

76

Barry snuffled and said, "Payback time." The boys stood and walked into the house. After a minute, Mark heard them go out the front door.

He turned to Laurie. "Did you see it, too?"

"Yeah. No wonder they can't put Traci's disappearance behind them. No wonder they wanted a feud with Hudson. How would you feel, if you had to live through that over and over again?" She paused. "Do you think they remember it after every time they see it?"

"Not clearly. Otherwise, they'd realize that something weird is happening to them. They probably think they just sit and talk, and imagine." He stood up. "Come on. I think they have enough of a lead."

He didn't *want* to follow the Red Chessmen any further, not now that there were so many of them. It seemed too dangerous. But he kept thinking about knives. The bloody blade in the vision. The ones in Barry's doodles. And especially, the butterfly knife in the Cooper boy's pocket. He was afraid that tonight was going to be the night when Laurie's brother and his friends actually tried to kill someone. If so, they had to be stopped.

The Red Chessmen kept to side streets and alleys. As they walked several blocks, the rows of homes gave way to businesses. After passing a shoe store, a newsstand, and a mall, they loped into a parking lot. The neon sign on the roof of the building beyond it said BOWL-A-ARAMA. Above the letters, a red ball knocked down white pins in a three-step animation. Below them, a hanging banner read, MEN'S SEMIFINALS THURS. NITE.

The Cooper High guys fanned out near the entrance, then hunkered down behind parked cars. Laurie and Mark stopped at the edge of the lot, behind a telephone pole. "They've set up an ambush," he whispered.

77

Laurie said, "How do they know any cadets are in there?"

"Maybe the same . . . *thing* that sent the vision tipped them off."

"Maybe." She frowned. "But how do they *think* they know?"

"Beats me. Could be that right now their minds are too messed up to question it. Anyway, it doesn't matter. Get to a phone and call the police. Tell them kids are hanging around out here. With luck, a cop will come and run them off before they get a chance to do any damage. Just don't give your name. It isn't safe to let anybody know you're mixed up in this."

"What are you going to do?"

"Keep watching. Stop them if I have to."

"How?"

"I don't know. Get going, and maybe I won't have to be creative."

"Okay. Be careful." She squeezed his hand, then hurried into the darkness.

Every few seconds, he peeked around the pole. The breeze raised goose bumps on his bare arms. His nerves buzzed with anxiety. Very shortly it seemed like Laurie had been gone an hour, though he knew it had really only been a couple minutes.

One of the Bowl-a-rama's glass doors swung open. His muscles tensed. Two girls came out and walked toward a yellow Isuzu parked beneath a lamppost. Just as Mark sighed in relief, the door opened a second time. Two guys carrying soda cups ambled into the night. One was wearing a Hudson uniform. Both had short hair.

As far as Mark knew, the two guys weren't Gray Chessmen. Maybe the evening's vision had left Barry and his friends so angry that they couldn't pass up a chance to hurt any cadet, because they got

78

ready to attack anyway.

But they weren't quite reckless enough to do it in front of witnesses. They waited while the girls climbed into the Isuzu. Mark realized that if he could pass himself off as another innocent bystander, he might be able to keep the would-be attackers from making their move.

He snatched off his glasses, stuck them in his pocket, and mussed his hair, then strode toward the Bowl-a-rama. He was thirty feet from the cadets when the yellow car started for the street.

"Hey, guys," he called. "What's happening?"

"Not much," said the cadet in uniform, smiling uncertainly. Mark noticed that his black tie was loose and crooked; Colonel Green wouldn't approve. "Do we know you?"

"No," Mark said, moving closer. "But do you want to bowl a couple of games?"

"We can't," the uniformed cadet said. "We have an errand to run before curfew. Some of our friends are still inside though."

The other cadet, a pug-nosed guy with a small purple birthmark below his hairline, frowned and said, "I think we do know you."

"Come on," Mark said. "Just one game." At last, he was just a few feet away from them. Close enough to speak softly and be heard. "You're in danger," he whispered. "Go back inside."

"What?" said the uniformed cadet.

"Keep your voice down!" Mark said. "You're in danger. Go inside."

"I *do* know you!" the boy with the birthmark exclaimed. "You're that McIntyre kid! The one that went crazy and trashed all that stuff!"

The Red Chessmen charged.

Sixteen

The two cadets gaped stupidly at the onrushing attackers. Mark shoved them backward. "Run!" he yelled.

The cadets scrambled back through the bowling alley door. Mark got inside on their heels. He prayed that the Red Chessmen wouldn't come in, but when he looked back, he saw that they were still charging. Something, the flight of their chosen victims or the sight of someone they thought was the worst of their enemies, had driven them wild.

Mark fumbled with the door's lock. He was an instant too slow. Barry and Roger plowed through the door. Mark reeled back, fighting to keep his balance. He was sure that if he fell, he'd never get up. The Cooper High guys would be all over him before he could.

A big, pot-bellied man with a gray-stubbled chin scrambled from behind the cash register, interposing himself between the Red Chessmen and their prey. "What's the matter with you?" he shouted. "You can't fight in here!"

Roger said, "Yes, we can," and knocked him out of the way. The man slammed headfirst into a wall-mounted bulletin board, then slumped unconscious to the floor.

But his interference had given Mark time to lengthen his lead. Crouched low, he scuttled away, taking advantage of every bit of cover.

Some of the bowling alley customers began to cry out, or hurry toward the exits. Meanwhile, Barry and his friends muscled their way through the crowd, shoving or swatting people aside. A couple of the Red Chessmen had luminous eyes. One looked like an ape in human disguise, hunched, with bandy legs and too-long arms. Roger's silver skull earring dangled from a pointed ear.

The Cooper guys split up to intercept all of the dozen or so cadets in sight. Most of the Hudson students tried to evade them. But Ken and Warren, the two Gray Chessmen present, charged, mad with a bloodlust of their own.

Because he'd started moving first, Mark reached the side exit ahead of the frightened bowlers. He was about to duck outside when a shriek of pain cut through the babble of dismay.

Mark stopped. No matter how scared he was, he couldn't just run while people were getting hurt. Fumbling to get his glasses back on, he darted to the foot of the first bowling lane and climbed on the scorer's chair. "I'm over here!" he shouted.

None of the Red Chessmen looked around. They must not have heard him over all the other noise.

He jumped down and grabbed a blue-speckled ball off the sweep. He swung it over his head, then hurled it down on the slick wooden floor. The huge crash got everyone's attention, and the clamor died.

"I'm the one you want!" Mark yelled. "*I* tore down your bleachers! *I* killed your stupid goat! Not them!" He swung his arm in a gesture that took in all the innocent cadets. "*Me!*"

The taunt worked. Three Red Chessmen kept fighting Ken and Warren, but the rest turned away from the boys they were stalking or mauling. Great, Mark thought grimly. Now all I have to do is keep them from killing me.

Since none of the Red Chessmen were within twenty feet of him, he'd hoped he could blend back into the crowd before any of his pursuers got a chance to attack. But unfortunately, he'd given them an idea. A Cooper guy with a flat-nosed face hefted a bowling ball in his oversized hand, then threw it like a baseball, his jacket splitting at the shoulder. Caught by surprise, Mark ducked just in time to keep from getting brained. The ball crashed into the cinder-block wall behind him.

An instant later, the air was full of balls. Mark flung himself down. As he dropped, one missile clipped his shoulder.

The flash of pain made him fear a bone was broken, but there was no time to worry about that now. He scrambled forward, lunging behind a plastic bench, then back into the milling crowd.

Now that he'd distracted Barry and his buddies, maybe it would be okay to sneak out, but now the exits were jammed. All Mark could do was keep moving and stay low.

The crow surged suddenly, jostling him sideways. His hip bumped painfully into a coin-operated pool table, and he was shoved to the edge of the game area, between the snack bar and the pro shop.

In front of him, two people fell as a Red Chessman pushed through the crowd. And this guy was *really* red, with fox-colored hair growing halfway down his chimpanzee forehead and bushy copper eyebrows that met above his nose. Mark's stomach turned when he saw what the transformed boy held in his red-furred hand — a cocked revolver.

Mark quickly snatched a cue stick off the pool table and swung it at the redhead's gun hand. The stick snapped in two. The revolver banged as it tumbled to the floor.

The redhead yelped and snatched at Mark with his other hand. Mark ducked, evading the grab, and slammed the butt of the stick against the Chessman's temple. The redhead grunted, staggered a step, and fell.

Gasping, his heart hammering, Mark supposed he should thank God that Chessmen didn't grow armor plating to go with their humongous muscles. Then something roared.

Mark whirled, then froze. Another Red Chessman, who looked exactly like the first, was running at him, and lifting a bowling pin like a club. The pin swept down. At the last possible instant, Mark jerked out of its way. Sidestepping, he rammed the end of the broken stick into the guy's kidney, then kicked the back of his knee. Bone snapped. The Chessman screamed and fell on top of his double.

As he picked up the bowling pin, Mark remembered Laurie mentioning Jim and Jerry Thomas. He wished she'd told him they were twins.

Something flashed at the edge of his vision. He jumped back. A blade flashed by an inch from his nose.

Barry shuffled forward, eyes glittering, the butterfly knife shining in his hand.

Mark faked a strike at the other boy's face, then tried to bash him across the wrist with the pin. Barry blocked the makeshift club with his other hand and the club fell out of Mark's hand. The next instant, Barry lunged and thrust. The Hudson student frantically leaped away, narrowly avoiding a stab in the stomach.

Mark knew he was in trouble. Except for the fever-ish light in his eyes, Barry didn't have the bestial look of most of the other Chessmen, but he was as strong as any of them. "Look," Mark said, "this is stupid. I didn't really kill your goat, and I'm not one of your enemies, either. Not anymore. I quit the gang."

"I don't believe you," Barry said. "And even if I did, you guys have to pay for Traci."

"I never even met her," Mark replied. "She disap-peared before I ever got here!"

Barry sprang.

Mark ducked one slash, parried another. The blade darted at his wrist, he snatched his arm back—

And pain blasted through his head. As he dropped to his knees, Mark realized he'd been sucker punched again. He'd been so busy watching the knife that he hadn't seen Barry's other hand coming.

The Red Chessman kicked him in the belly, smash-ing the remaining strength out of his body. He would have fallen on his face, but Barry grabbed his collar and hauled him to his feet, then pressed the point of the knife against his throat.

"Don't hurt him!" a girl cried.

Mark couldn't move his head for fear of being cut. He shifted his eyes. Laurie was standing five feet away. She'd come back after phoning the cops.

"What are you doing here?" Barry demanded. "Are you *with* this guy?" Mark sensed that if she said yes, the Chessman would stab him instantly.

"No!" she said. "I came to bowl. What the heck are you *doing?*"

Barry said, "We have to get these guys."

"Don't be stupid," Laurie pleaded. "If you kill him, it'll ruin your life. Hurt Mom and Dad. And me."

The rage in Barry's face gave way to confusion. Evi-dently, he loved his sister enough that, even sunk in a

Chessman's rage, he still cared what she thought.

But he didn't take the knife away, so maybe he didn't care enough to let Mark go. The cadet waited to see if he was going to live or die. Suddenly, sirens wailed outside.

Barry snarled and threw Mark to the floor. He and his friends, all but the disabled twins, ran for the exits, which were finally clear. In a moment, they were gone.

Wheezing, Mark climbed to his hands and knees. Laurie crouched beside him. "Are you all right?" she asked.

"Do I look all right? Help me up." She gripped his arm and hoisted him to his feet. He took a step and managed not to fall; his strength was trickling back. "I've got to go before the cops come in. Don't squeal on anybody. I've got a feeling these weren't all the Red Chessmen, and if you help put this bunch in jail, the others might come after you." He hobbled away.

As he passed the redheads, the fallen revolver caught his eye. He picked it up and stuck it in his belt. Reaching the side door, he peered out warily. All clear. With his stomach and shoulder aching, his breath hissing through gritted teeth, he staggered into the darkness.

Seventeen

The next evening Mark was waiting in the woods again for Laurie. This time he was wearing his Hudson uniform. He had carefully hidden his other clothes under some bushes nearby. When a hand fell on Mark's epaulet, he squawked and jerked around.

Holding his supper bag in her hand, Laurie grinned. "Got you," she said.

He glared at her. "Life is scary enough right now without you sneaking up on me."

"Sorry," she said. "I saw you lurking behind your bush like Daniel Boone or somebody, and I couldn't resist. I didn't want to stay on the path tonight. There are too many kids on their way to the Nightmare Club. I was afraid somebody would pass me, then notice that I never got there. So I circled around that way." She pointed.

"I'm sorry I snapped at you," he said. "I'm glad to see you. I was worried that Barry would keep you away."

"I think he suspects that I did go to the Bowl-a-rama with you, but he's in a bind. He can't stand guard over me and run around with his buddies, too. How are you? I was scared that you needed to go to a hospital . . ."

"So was I, but I'm just bruised." She handed him

the sack. Opening it, he discovered two hot dogs in foil wrappers, a container of cole slaw, and a plastic fork.

"Oh, yeah, here's the penlight you asked for."

"Thanks. Tell me . . . the news. You don't know what a pain it is, hiding alone in a room all day with no idea of what's going on."

"Well, let's see. Some of the cadets at the bowling alley got beat up pretty bad, but they'll be okay. The Thomas twins are under arrest. But the cops haven't identified any other Red Chessmen—I guess because of the confusion, and the way most of their faces changed. I wish I could have told on them. The story in the newspaper said the 'assailants' were wearing Halloween masks."

"Crap," Mark said. "I was hoping the whole goon squad would wind up in detention."

"Tell me about it. I'd give anything to have Barry safely locked up."

"The whole town ought to be locked up," Mark said irritably. "No kid should be allowed out after sunset."

"People are upset," she said, "but they don't know we're headed for a wave of murders. They just see a handful of punks making trouble, worse than other years but nothing too special. So they're not going to sit on every teenager in the Hollow."

"I know," he sighed.

"What are *we* going to do tonight? Are you in uniform again for a special reason? Are we going to tail some of the Chessmen again?"

"And jump out and stop them if they try to hurt somebody?" His shoulder and stomach twinged at the thought. "Jeez, do I *look* like Batman? Next time, I'd get killed for sure. No, I still think we need to pull the plug on whatever's *causing* this garbage."

"Fine, but how?"

"Last night we found out that the Red Chessmen's craziness is tied to the idea that Wes Lombard killed Traci Elmore. Suppose we prove he didn't. Maybe they'd snap back to normal."

Laurie cocked her head. "How do you know he didn't?"

"I don't," Mark said. He unwrapped a hot dog and gobbled a bite. "But if Wes did murder her, it was awfully convenient for who-, or whatever, wanted to control Barry and his buddies. Isn't it more likely that the controller killed Traci *and* Wes, and his mind-movie is a lie?"

"Maybe," Laurie said. "But the Chessmen won't believe that without evidence. And search parties have already combed the woods."

"But the searchers didn't know about Toby Gregson and his evil spirit."

"Come again?"

"What if Toby, what's the word, *communed* with the spirit in a particular part of the woods? What if, for some reason, that's where Wes and Traci got killed? If we went over that bit of ground with a fine-tooth comb, we might find the evidence."

"Maybe," Laurie said. "But we don't know where it is."

"Greg does. Maybe he has a map or directions written down. He might need them, if he only visits the Hollow once a century. Anyway, I'm going to sneak back into Hudson, go through his stuff, and find out."

"So that's why you're wearing your uniform." She shook her head. "I don't know, this sounds like a real long shot. But I admit I don't have a better idea, so let's do it."

Eighteen

Mark stepped from behind his tree, jumped, grabbed the top of the wall, and pulled himself up, doing his best to ignore the twinge in his shoulder. The windows in the building ahead were dark, as they should have been a half an hour after taps.

"Be careful," Laurie whispered. He wished she were going with him. But it was a bad idea. A guy who spotted Mark might not recognize him, or realize he was doing anything illicit, even though everyone was supposed to be in bed. But if anybody saw a girl, he'd know immediately that something strange was going on.

The cadet jumped down and scurried toward the academy. To his right, something scuffed.

Mark dove behind a bush. A beam of light cut through the space where he'd just been. A man with a billy club and walkie-talkie clipped to his belt strode by, close enough to touch.

Terrific, Mark thought, shivering. No doubt concerned by the recent vandalism and violence, Colonel Green had hired security guards. The teenager wondered how many were patrolling. At least two, or the one he'd seen wouldn't have a radio.

Mark gave the man a minute to get farther away, then sneaked on. When he was a little more than half-way across the lawn, another flashlight shone in his direction. He ducked behind a tree. The beam swept along a flowerbed, then went out. He heard the rent-a-cop move away, toward the front of the building.

The cadet slunk to one of the side doors. It wouldn't open. Obviously, a school that hired security guards would also lock its doors.

He started working his way down the wall. Maybe someone had forgotten to fasten a window.

On his eighth try, one rose a fraction of an inch, stopped, squeaked up three more inches and froze again.

He pushed. The window wouldn't budge. Footsteps trudged in his direction.

He almost ran. But suppose the guard noticed the window part way open, shut it, and locked it. Then Mark might never get inside.

So he pushed harder. When the window still didn't move, he tried to pull it down. It wouldn't close, either. The footsteps grew louder.

Gritting his teeth, Mark shoved as hard as he could. The window resisted another second, then shot up. The cadet scrambled inside, yanked it down, crouched, and peered out. The security guard, a black silhouette with a flame-tipped cigarette in his mouth, trudged past a moment later. He obviously hadn't heard a thing.

Panting, his heart beating rapidly, Mark looked around. He was in a classroom. A pull-down map lolled across the chalkboard like a tongue.

He tiptoed to the door. Cracked it open. The corridor was empty. So he slunk on. The gun in his belt nudged him in the back. And suddenly he thought, maybe I'm making this too complicated. Why should

I try to figure all this garbage out? When I get to Greg's room, I can just shoot him. *That* ought to stop the Gray Chessmen.

But he knew he wouldn't. Sure, he could fist fight, even though it always scared him. Bullies often liked to pick on the new kid, the guy with no friends. Mark had learned the hard way how to defend himself. But no way could he murder anyone in cold blood, not even a three hundred year-old master of black magic.

Besides, as things stood, Mark wasn't in that much legal trouble. If he turned himself in now, he could go through the punishment pretty quickly, and soon get back to a normal existence. But if he wound up accused of murder, his life would be ruined. He'd probably spend the rest of it in prison.

He skulked up a staircase to the sophomore barracks. The air smelled of disinfectant, evidence that the cleanup detail had been getting ready for tomorrow morning's inspection. One guy was snoring, two others were whispering. The musical fallout from somebody's headphones murmured faintly. For some reason, it made him imagine ghosts having a party.

Tenth-graders, like juniors, were supposed to bunk four to a room. But Greg had his own. As Mark cracked open the door, he wondered if the warlock had used magic to make the housing officer put him by himself. It would be one way to guard his secrets.

The cadet thought the room smelled musty, but it could have been his imagination. A motionless form, cocooned in blankets, lay on one of the lower bunks. Atop the dresser sat a first baseman's mitt, a jar half full of pennies, and a photo of a smiling man and woman, supposedly Greg's parents. Mark wondered who the people really were. Maybe the picture had come with the frame.

He eased the door shut, then crept toward Greg's

desk, his ears straining to catch any movement. The room stayed silent.

In fact, it was *too* silent. He didn't even hear breathing. Suddenly sure he was alone, he gently turned back Greg's covers. There was nothing under them but pillows.

Of course. The Gray Chessmen were on another raid. If Mark could manage to get past security guards and locked doors, then it followed that Greg, with his magic powers, could sneak by them, too. Trying not to think about the harm they might be doing, Mark took out the penlight Laurie had brought for him and began to search the room.

There was nothing in the desk but school stuff. Mark smiled wryly to discover that Greg was aceing American History. It figured, since he *lived* through most of it. He raked through garments folded in the dresser, then the ones hanging in the closet. Next he lifted battered leather valises off the shelf above the desk.

They weren't locked. Perhaps at some point in their years, decades, or centuries of service, Greg had lost the keys. Kneeling among them, the penlight clenched between his teeth, Mark examined them by sight and touch. Running his fingers over the inside of the largest, he felt a bulge. He groped around, fumbling open a hidden compartment.

Inside was a large, thin book with a flaking cover. It looked and smelled so old that he was almost afraid to handle it, for fear that it would crumble into dust. On its ragged parchment pages were lines of faded script, and geometric designs incorporating Latin and Hebrew writing.

Mark grinned in satisfaction. Then he froze. Behind him, something jingled.

92

Nineteen

Mark jerked around. He could see nothing, but he *sensed* something hurtling at his head. He flung himself to the side. Glass shattered, and metal clattered, the sound of coins spilling across a hard surface.

His heart thumping, he grabbed the penlight and lashed it back and forth, searching desperately for whoever had thrown the jar at him. He still didn't see anything. Something soft slid around his throat.

He dropped the light and tore at whatever was choking him. He felt cloth and a hard, round button. Another length of fabric coiled around his right wrist. Countless pennies and shards of glass, gleaming softly in the starlight from the window, floated into the air.

And then Mark understood. Greg's magic book had magic protection.

He threw himself down. Coins and glass hurtled over him like a swarm of angry wasps. Shirts, coats, and pairs of pants hovered around him, trying to strangle and bind him. In the closet, wire hangers jangled as other garments slipped free.

Mark's sight began to dim, warning him he was close to passing out. In the moment it took the pennies and jar fragments to retarget him, he forced his fingers under the sleeve that was choking him, gouging his skin in the process. He yanked with all his might and the cloth ripped away.

As he gasped in a breath, the pennies and smashed pieces of glass pelted him. This time he couldn't get out of the way. He just squeezed his eyes shut, lowered his head, and threw up his arms. The missiles stung.

Mark started to bolt for the door, then realized he was forgetting the book. He grabbed it from the valise, stuck it under his arm, and jumped up. A suitcase snapped shut on his foot. He crashed back to the floor, and pain jolted through his shoulder.

Another valise floated toward his head, gnashing open and shut like jaws. He batted it away. Kicking frantically, his foot jerked free, minus its shoe.

He lurched up, almost fell again when a pair of striped uniform trousers slithered around his lower legs. By the time he pulled them off, the dresser had slid in front of the door.

Mark tried to shove it away. It resisted. The struggle rocked it, sending the framed photo crashing to the floor. The first baseman's glove flew at Mark and swatted him on the nose.

An instant later, a barrage of coins and glass hit him in the back. He cried out at the unexpected pain. A valise dove from above, nearly catching his head inside itself. He shoved the dresser again, but it still wouldn't move. Beyond the door, voices babbled. Someone knocked.

Mark whirled the other way.

A valise swooped at his shins. He bounded over it. A strip of cloth squirmed over his glasses, blinding him.

He didn't stop to tear it off. Some instinct warned him that if he did, the rest of the animated objects would take him down. He sprinted two more strides, whipped his free arm in front of his face, and leaped.

He seemed to hang in the air for a long time. He was afraid he'd jumped too soon, that he was about to fall to the floor. Then he slammed into the window.

The glass exploded. Mark tumbled. His shoeless foot hit the ground, and he sat down hard on the grass. Scraps of window showered around him.

He ripped off the writhing black necktie that had blindfolded him, kicked away a white shirt that was trying to tie his ankles. A garden hose reared in an S curve, then struck at him like a snake.

Mark rolled sideways. The brass nozzle thudded repeatedly on the ground. Checking to make sure he still had the book, the cadet scrambled up and ran.

Before he'd gone five paces, a rake that was leaning against a tree floated into the air, then spun in front of him.

My God, Mark thought, it's never going to stop. Not till I'm dead, or I throw the book away.

But he couldn't. It was too important, and he'd gone through too much to get it.

The rake flew at him, chopping at his head. He tried to dodge. The hose jabbed him in the back, knocking him toward the gleaming tines.

Mark dove, rolled under the rake and back to his feet. Then he bolted. When he glanced back, the tool was streaking after him, faster than he could run.

But just as it entered striking range, it tumbled out of the air. Apparently the magic had finally run out of gas.

Gasping, his glasses smeary with sweat, Mark slowed to a stumbling trot. He could hardly believe he was going to get away. Unfortunately he wasn't in the clear yet. In front of him now stood a big man with a club. Mark had forgotten all about the security guards.

"You stop right there," said the guard, striding forward.

Mark was sure he was too exhausted to outrun him. Then he remembered the revolver. Maybe it would scare the man away. The teenager reached under the back of his coat and tried to jerk the gun out of his pants.

It caught on something. He yanked with all his might. It still wouldn't pull free. The guard reached for Mark's shoulder.

Mark bellowed and lunged at him, caught him by surprise and knocked him down.

The guard yelled curses and threats as he rose to chase him, but Mark got to the wall first. He leaped over and saw Laurie jump out of hiding. Together they disappeared into the thick, dark woods.

Twenty

Gray squirrels bounded along the branches. The sky was blue, the leaves, green, red, and yellow. After keeping an owl's hours for the past two days, Mark was keenly aware of the beauty of the sunlit woods. He would have enjoyed it even more if his bruises and cuts had stopped twinging. And if he weren't worried about somebody seeing him.

But that was an unavoidable risk. He and Laurie couldn't search effectively at night.

The brown-haired girl brushed a gnat away from her face. She'd gone home last night and had come back early this morning with his breakfast. Since today was Saturday, she could stay with him all day. "We've come pretty far north," she said.

Dressed again in his jeans and tee-shirt headbanger disguise Mark opened the stolen book. The musty-smelling volume had taken a beating during his escape. The back cover had fallen off, and most of the pages had come loose from the binding. Fortunately, the writing and sketches were still legible.

Mark pointed to the crude map. "Do you think we're north of this bend in the river?"

"Probably not."

"Then the 'spirit's domain' should still be ahead."

"That's how it looks, but I don't think Traci and Wes would have walked this far."

"Maybe that's what everyone thought, and why nobody found them. They might have gone a long way if something lured them. Or forced them. Let's hike another mile. If we don't spot a 'golden stone' or any of the other landmarks Toby wrote about by then, we'll swing west and work our way back south."

"Whatever you say, mighty hunter."

They walked on, holding hands when the going permitted. A cut under Mark's left wrist band began to itch. He tolerated it as long as he could, then pulled off the studded cuff and scratched.

"Darn it," Laurie said, "our problems should be over."

"How so?"

"Last night, somebody set fire to a Cooper High boy's house." Remembering his dream, Mark winced, even though she'd already told him everyone had escaped this blaze unhurt. "Meanwhile, you woke the academy. Somebody should have noticed Greg and the other Gray Chessmen were missing. Somebody should have been able to tie them in to the arson. They should be in jail now."

"All I can figure is, somehow Greg's magic kept them out of trouble," Mark said. He started to buckle the wrist band back on, then decided not to bother. After his high-profile visit to the Bowl-a-rama, his townie disguise was probably useless anyway. He stuffed the band in his jeans pocket. "Maybe it made Colonel Green *think* he saw them, or forget he didn't. Anyway, you and I are still stuck with the problem."

Laurie smiled crookedly. "Isn't it nice to feel important." Her brown eyes widened. "Look!"

Mark turned. Ahead of them stood a rock as tall as a man. Its tapering shape and dull yellow color made it look like a rotting fang. "Toby's 'golden stone!' " the cadet exclaimed.

"Yeah. Detective time."

They moved slowly forward, peering about, searching for the evidence they needed. Nearing the rock, Mark noticed the air felt cooler. Hesitantly, he touched the stone's weathered surface. It seemed colder than it should have been. Thinking of the chess pieces, he shivered. But perhaps the trees around the rock kept it shaded from the sun.

He wondered if he'd feel warmer after they worked their way past. He didn't. A chill breeze began to blow. The color bled out of the day. He glanced up. A cloud was oozing across the sun.

Laurie said, "All of a sudden, this *feels* like a dark spirit's home."

"Since Greg's magic is real, I guess that, in a way, it is. We just have to hope that people like us can't bump into it, any more than you run into angels when you go to church."

They began seeing dead and twisted trees like the ones around the Nightmare Club. Some had cancerous gnarls of bark that looked like anguished faces. Toby Gregson's notes mentioned "souls sealed in wood," and Mark had wondered what the reference meant. Now that he'd seen, he was sorry to have his curiosity satisfied.

Someone sobbed.

Mark whirled toward Laurie, but she wasn't crying. She looked as startled as he was.

The sound came again, through the bare, stunted trees ahead. A girl's voice wailed, "Oh, Wes! Oh, Wes!"

"I know that voice!" Laurie said. "It's Traci!"

"After all this time?" asked Mark. "It can't be."

"I'm telling you, it's her. Come on!"

"All right," he said, "but let's sneak up. Who knows what's going on."

They crept forward, crouching low, using the trees for cover. In a minute, they came to a brushy hill so steep it was almost a cliff.

Mark's ears told him the crying was coming from the foot of the slope. But there was no one there. His mouth went dry. "Jeez," he whispered, "is it another ghost?"

"I'm going to call her," Laurie said. "We have to." Mark nodded reluctantly. "Traci!"

The shout echoed from the hillside. The weeping stopped, but no one answered.

"Traci!" Laurie repeated. "It's Laurie Frank! I came to help you!"

For a few seconds, there was silence. Then the other girl's voice said, "Laurie?"

"Yes! I can hear you, but I can't see you. Where are you?"

"In a cave! There are bushes in front of the opening."

"Can you come out?" Laurie asked.

"No," Traci sobbed. "I'm tied up."

"Keep talking," Laurie said. "Your voice will lead me to you." She and Mark hurried to the bottom of the hill.

"At first, I screamed my throat raw, every day," Traci blubbered. "Nobody came. I thought nobody ever would."

Laurie pulled a clump of brush apart, exposing the brown soil beneath. "Who did this to you?"

"Wes," Laurie said. "He went crazy. He said he knew it was the only way to keep me from dumping him. And I loved him so *much!*"

Baffled, Mark shook his head. How did Wes and his captive survive out here? And exactly how did the former cadet's craziness tie in with Greg and the Chessmen?

Well, he supposed he and Laurie would figure everything out eventually. For now, the important thing was to get Traci back to town and show Barry and his friends she was alive.

The cadet shoved a thorny bush aside. Behind it was a crack. If he turned sideways, he'd have just enough room to squirm through.

He peered. Listened. He couldn't see Traci, but he could tell her sniffling was coming from inside. He turned to Laurie. "Found her."

He wriggled through the opening. Laurie followed. The space inside was just wide enough for them to walk shoulder to shoulder, just high enough for Mark to stand straight. The dim sunlight, blocked by the brush and their bodies, only shone a few feet ahead.

"It's all right," Laurie called, taking a new penlight out of her jacket pocket. "We're in the cave. We're coming." She and Mark moved forward.

A tide of icy darkness swept over them. For an instant, Mark was sure he'd gone blind. Then the little flashlight shone again. But the faint glow behind him went out.

Twenty-one

Mark and Laurie whirled. A mass of darkness blocked the cave mouth. Four slits of dull red—eyes, Mark realized—shone near the top. The beam of the light in Laurie's trembling hand jittered over it, vaguely revealing shoulders that extended from wall to wall, and a three-fingered fist the size of a watermelon.

Mark was terrified. And furious at himself. He'd sensed something was wrong and *still* led Laurie into a trap. He dropped the book of magic, snatched the revolver out of the back of his jeans and pointed it. The barrel shook as much as Laurie's flashlight.

The creature laughed, at first in a girlish giggle. Gradually the noise grew deeper and louder, till it sounded like iron gates clashing shut. His ears throbbing, Mark cringed.

Finally, the hideous noise died. "Bullets and blades can't hurt me," the dark thing rumbled.

"What are you?" Laurie quavered.

"You know. Toby's—or do you call him Greg?—patron spirit. And I know you, too, from watching the town. What an unexpected pleasure to meet you

102

face to face. I'm glad you touched my boundary stone and woke me."

Mark winced, hating himself even though there was no way he could have known.

"What do you want?" asked Laurie.

"Mainly," the spirit said, "I want to make sure you don't spoil my game."

"I don't understand," said Mark, even though he thought he was beginning to. But if he kept the spirit talking, maybe he could think of a way to escape.

"No?" asked the thing, its eyes smoldering. "It's simple enough. My race hates yours. We'd like to stamp you out. With the powers at our command, it ought to be easy. But unfortunately we are too often confined to other planes of existence. Or, as is my case, we are chained to a particular patch of ground. It drains us to strike at someone far away. So occasionally we lend a measure of our power to an evil mortal. Unlike us, such a man can move freely among you, doing harm."

"And that's where warlocks come from," Laurie said.

"And certain other night-gangers," the spirit said. "Now, two hundred years ago, there dwelled hereabouts a boy named Toby Gregson. He was unprincipled, avid for riches, and obsessed with the worry that he, like the rest of your breed, must one day die. Somehow he picked up a bit of occult lore, enough to find his way here by dowsing ley lines — using a divining rod to follow the paths of mystic force that run through the earth, much as old-time well-diggers located water.

"Of course, he came to beg for eternal youth and sorcerous might. But before I weakened myself by granting his wishes, I wanted to be sure he was worthy. That he possessed the talent, cunning, and ruthlessness to wreak great ill. To test him, I devised a competition.

"I'd lend him magic, and he'd use it to madden, strengthen, and dominate some of the white people in the Hollow. Meanwhile, I'd do the same to certain Indians, and we'd pit the two groups against one another. If I lost more men than he did, then he could keep the power and his youth for a hundred years."

"But after that, he'd start to age, wouldn't he?" Mark guessed. That must be why Greg sometimes shriveled when he strained himself using his powers. His unnatural vitality must have started to run out. "He'd have to come back and play again."

"Exactly," the spirit said. "So I could make sure he hadn't gone soft or stupid. And so one day, when his luck ran out, he'd die. I loathe him as much as the rest of your kind. I wasn't about to let him live *forever.*

"I think you know the rest. He's won twice now. In that first game two hundred years ago, his whites bested my red men in battle. In the second, his cadets drugged the orphanage supper, then set fire to the annex where my lads lay sleeping. I never thought that was quite sporting. Well, we'll see what happens this time. My pawns are ready to kill. They'll launch what I hope will be a decisive attack tonight."

"One of those 'pawns' is my brother!" Laurie shrilled. Now she sounded as angry as she was afraid.

"With luck, he'll survive to mourn you," the spirit said. "Though he may find he's lost the capacity. Up to a point, a corrupted dupe can recover his humanity. But once he's committed murder, darkness takes root in his soul."

The spirit hitched its shoulders. "Well, this has been nice. Sometimes I go for decades with no one to talk to. But enough conversation is enough."

"Wait!" Mark cried. "We don't want to die any more than Greg! Let us make the same deal he did! Then you'll have three warlocks instead of one!"

"An interesting idea," the dark thing said. "If you meant it. But I can see into your heart, and I see that loneliness has made you strong-willed and independent. Even to save your life, you could never acknowledge the absolute authority of any master, let alone one whose inclinations run utterly contrary to your own. So I know your offer is only a trick." It stepped forward.

Mark jumped in front of Laurie. "Run!" he screamed, and started shooting.

The spirit lunged, moving impossibly fast for something that so nearly filled the tunnel. A wave of freezing darkness washed over Mark, as if he'd been pulled inside the creature's body. A rock-hard hand grabbed him by the shoulder and slammed him into the wall. Dazed, he fell, the revolver tumbling from his fingers.

When he came to his senses, the creature was dragging him out of the cave. Somehow, its massive body slipped through the crack. The boy looked back. The beam of the fallen penlight shone on Laurie's face. Her eyes were closed, and blood welled from her scalp. He wailed her name, but she didn't stir.

"I'm afraid you can't perish together," the spirit said. "Even though you've shaken off Toby's control, the rules say you're still part of the game. If you lose your life, I score a point." Now Mark understood why Greg hadn't let the Gray Chessmen drown him.

"But I do not score if I slay you myself," explained the spirit. "Then the whole contest would deteriorate into my opponent and me slinging death spells about. And that's not a game at all! You have to die by mortal hands. So I'm going to imprison you outside. Tomorrow one of my minions will dispose of you. But there's no reason I shouldn't butcher Laurie myself. If it's any consolation to you, your end will almost certainly be less painful than hers."

Mark thrashed, but couldn't break his captor's grip. The creature hauled him through the brier. The thorns ripped him. The daylight made him squint.

As the spirit pulled him across the ground, its body began to steam. Mark guessed that, even filtered through the cloud cover, the sun was hurtful to it. He struggled madly, but still couldn't tear himself free.

The spirit swung him over its head and dashed him to the ground. The shock jolted pain through his limbs and bounced his glasses off. As he groggily rolled onto his back, a weight fell on his ankles. He passed out.

Twenty-two

Mark awoke thrashing. When his eyes popped open, he was looking straight at the sun, which had come out from behind the clouds. The glare of light startled the panic out of him.

He was thirsty. Much of his body ached, though his feet were numb. Blinking, he peered around, spied his glasses, and fumbled them on. That accomplished, he saw that he was still where the spirit had thrown him, with an oblong boulder lying across his ankles.

He sat up and tried to roll the stone off. It seemed heavier than it had any right to be, as if the spirit had increased its weight with magic. At any rate, it only shifted a fraction of an inch, just enough to jab fresh pain through his legs. Bark faces watched from the twisted trees. Before, he'd thought they looked like they were in agony. Now, they seemed to be leering.

He tried to drag his legs from under the rock. They wouldn't come. He called for help, a puny croak. No one answered.

Which meant he was trapped. For a moment, he thought he was going to cry.

Then he scowled, disgusted with himself. You

107

can't give up, he thought. People's lives are in danger. *Think* of something.

He tried to. Meanwhile, the sun crept across the sky. His throat grew drier. Flies buzzed around him, as if he were already dead.

When an idea finally came, he hated himself for not thinking of it before. Sitting up again, he clawed at the earth around his ankles.

The dirt seemed as hard as iron. He couldn't even scratch it.

Once again, he nearly caved in to despair. But it occurred to him that, though his bare hands couldn't do the job, tools might. He took the wrist band out of his pocket and chopped at the soil with the buckle. When some broke loose, he scooped it away.

It was the hardest work he'd ever done. His back ached with the strain of sitting up. Even after he wrapped his cramping hand in his tee-shirt, the buckle cut into his flesh. Gradually, the makeshift tool bent and lost its edge. After a while, he switched to his second band, and later, to his belt buckle.

As he dug, fears tortured him. What if the spirit came back to check on him? What if the belt buckle crumpled into uselessness before he ran out of dirt?

But luck was with Mark. After what seemed an eternity, his lower legs had dropped in a hole, while the ground supported the weight of the stone.

Panting, Mark squirmed backward. He stood up and fell down again, because he couldn't balance. He pulled off his sneakers and rubbed his feet, wincing at the stabbing pains of returning circulation.

When he felt able to walk, he put his shoes and grimy, tattered shirt back on, rose, and turned toward the spirit's cave. A spasm of terror made him shake.

I can't go in there, he thought. If I do, the spirit will catch me again. And Laurie's already dead anyway.

But he didn't *know* that. So, holding in a whimper, he skulked forward.

As he neared the brush in front of the entrance, he strained his ears. He heard nothing.

He pushed the brier aside, cringing when it rustled. Nothing shot out at him, so he peeked inside.

Except for a smear of blood, the revolver, and the penlight, still splashing illumination across the floor, the cave mouth was empty. Evidently, the spirit had taken Greg's book. Mark squirmed in and picked up the gun and flashlight.

The firearm smelled of burnt gunpowder. He checked to see how many shots he'd fired. Three, evidently, since there were two left. He tiptoed farther into the cave, flashlight in one hand, gun in the other, even though the weapon hadn't helped before.

He rounded one bend, then another, fearful each time that the spirit was lurking just beyond. The cave widened. In its center yawned a pit.

Mark shone the penlight over the edge. The girl at the bottom squawked and recoiled.

It was Laurie, alive! His stupidity hadn't killed her after all!

At least not yet. It still might if the spirit heard them trying to escape. He shushed her and whispered, "It's me!"

"Thank God!" she said, blinking in the light. Her forehead was caked with dried blood. "I thought you were dead!"

"I thought you were." He played the light around the pit. It looked about nine or ten feet deep. Two withered corpses, one in a rusty-spotted Cooper High cheerleader's sweater and the other in a tattered, equally bloodstained cadet uniform, lay on the floor. Traci Elmore and Wes Lombard, he assumed.

"The spirit said it was going back to sleep, but that it would be back for me at sunset. I guess even underground, night is its natural time."

"A break at last," Mark said. "Can you climb up?"

"No," Laurie said. "The walls are slippery with mud. I keep falling back."

"All right." He lay on his stomach, gripped the edge of the hole with one hand, and reached down with the other. "Take my hand." Standing on tiptoe, she was just able to reach it. "Now climb, and I'll lift."

She clambered upward. Teeth gritting, he pulled. Whenever her free hand and flailing feet lost their hold, he felt as if his arm was tearing out of its socket. For an instant, he was sure her weight was about to drag him down. Then she grabbed the edge and hauled herself to safety.

"Let's get out of here," she wheezed.

As they started toward the cave mouth, he noticed she was hobbling. By the time they passed the yellow stone, the limp had gotten worse. When the fang-shaped rock was out of sight, he raised his hand and they stumbled to a halt. "I think it's safe to rest now," he panted.

Laurie nodded. "Right. We're off its 'patch of ground.' "

"What happened to your leg?"

"I sprained it when the spirit threw me into the hole. My head hurts, too, and I'm seeing double."

Guilt wrung Mark's heart. "I hate myself for

110

bringing you here."

"Don't be stupid," she said. "I was willing to risk my butt to save other people's lives, especially since one of them is Barry's. Now that we know what happened to Traci and Wes, maybe we can stop this, provided you get back to the Hollow before dark."

He blinked. "Provided *I* get back?"

"I can't travel fast enough. You look pretty chewed up, but you seem to be moving okay. So it's up to you."

"But I can't leave you. You need a doctor."

"If we screw this up, a bunch of kids are going to need funerals. Don't worry about me. Go."

He realized she was right. There was no other way. He hugged her, then jogged south.

Twenty-three

A brown paper bag in his hand, Mark prowled the shopping center sidewalk, searching for Barry. Though he had washed up outside of town in an Aamco station's men's room, he still felt dirty, ragged, and beat up. He kept worrying that someone would stare at him, recognize him, and call the police.

At first when he had gotten back to town, Mark had considered warning the police that the Red Chessmen were planning to attack their rivals tonight. But since everyone thought he was crazy, he doubted he'd be believed. The call might even inspire the cops to look for him harder.

Instead, he had phoned the Frank home and asked to speak to Barry. Luckily Mrs. Frank told him that her son had driven to Cooper Plaza. Mark rushed there, only to realize that finding one guy in a shopping center on a busy Saturday afternoon was like finding a needle in a haystack.

Frustrated, he studied the bustling crowd. He'd figured out that his best hope of spotting Barry was to watch the row of storefronts, but in this mob, he could still miss him.

Four teenagers came out of the recessed entrance to the Plaza Cinema 4. Mark slunk closer. None of them was Barry.

The cadet looked around some more. From the corner of his eye, he caught a glint of red, but when he turned it was gone.

Probably his imagination. But maybe not, so he hurried forward, dodging off the curb to get around a woman in a motorized wheelchair.

When he stepped into the fire lane, he saw Barry, slouching down the sidewalk in a shiny red-and-white Cooper High jacket. The cadet darted after him, stopping just out of arm's reach. "Hi," he said.

Barry turned. For a second, he looked like a normal kid. Then his eyes began to glitter. "You," he said.

"You have to come with me." Mark said quickly. "Laurie's hurt. She needs help."

"What do you mean?" asked Barry. "How do you know about it? What was she doing with you?"

"At this point, does it matter? I'm telling you, she's *hurt*. We have to get her to a doctor."

The Cooper High student sneered. "Yeah, right. If she was really hurt, you'd get an ambulance."

"No. Because if I make contact with the authorities, I'm liable to wind up in jail."

"Well, the only way I'll go is with some of my friends. 'Cause I think you're trying to sucker me into a trap."

"Sorry," Mark said. If he took Barry and other Red Chessmen, too, they'd wind up rat-packing him for sure. "You *have* to come." He gripped the revolver inside the bag, flashed it, then tucked it out of sight again.

"Don't be stupid," said Barry. "You won't get away with this."

"Maybe not," Mark said, "but I will shoot you if you give me any crap. Take me to your car."

"I walked."

"That's not what your mom said. Move."

As they crossed the parking lot, Mark was terrified that someone would notice the odd way he was carrying the bag, or Barry's flushed, furious face. But nobody did. Evidently, most people only saw what they expected to see.

The Frank car was a white LeBaron convertible. The top was down. Mark glanced around, making sure no one was passing within earshot. "Empty your pockets."

Scowling, Barry set his keys, wallet, comb, a handful of pennies and dimes, the butterfly knife, and the wooden knight on the vehicle's trunk. Mark dropped the blade and the chess piece down a storm grate. "You can take back the rest," he said. "And then you're going to take me for a drive. Get on Old Wilson Highway and go north." He'd studied a map at the Amoco gas station to determine what road ran closest to the spirit's lair.

"Where did you guys get your chess pieces, anyway?" Mark asked, as the car pulled onto the street.

Barry blinked. "Jim and Jerry found them on their patio."

"And you didn't think that was weird." Mark sighed. "No, of course you didn't. When the magic has you under its spell, you can't think straight."

"Magic," the larger boy said, sneering. "You really are crazy."

"Maybe. With the things that keep happening, sometimes I wonder. Turn here."

Outside town, their route ran through rolling

farmland till they reached the proper turnoff into the woods. Past that point, the twisting road was narrow. Trees pressed close on either side, all but blocking out the sun. They stopped seeing other traffic.

Barry's jaw clenched, and his fingers kneaded the steering wheel. "What are you waiting for?" he asked. "There aren't any witnesses anymore."

Mark had decided to stop trying to reason with his captive until he showed Barry the corpses. But Barry looked so wild all of a sudden that Mark had to attempt to calm him down.

"I swear, I'm not planning to hurt you," said Mark. "What I said back at Cooper Plaza was the truth. Not the whole truth, but honest as far as it went. Laurie really is hurt—"

Barry's eyes blazed. "What did you do to her?"

"Nothing!"

"First Traci and now *my sister!*" Suddenly, the Red Chessman stamped on the gas pedal. The LeBaron hurtled toward a sharp bend in the road.

"Slow down!" screamed Mark, pulling the gun out of the bag.

The driver laughed. "Make me." He jerked the wheel.

Twenty-four

The car spun, lashing Mark against the door. He didn't mean to shoot, but the gun went off anyway, blasting a hole in the windshield.

The LeBaron hit something and bounced. Mark was afraid he'd be thrown out, but his seat belt snapped tight and held him. Landing on two wheels, the car rolled onto its side. Then it skidded nose first into an oak, the crash echoing through the woods.

Dazed, Mark shook his head, surprised to find he was still in one piece. He was on the side of the car that was on the ground. Barry hung above him, head lolling, arm dangling, a round silver airbag pressing against his chest.

Mark fumbled his safety belt open and squirmed out of the car. When he got up and checked, he saw it wasn't burning, so he knelt beside Barry and gently shook his shoulder. "Are you okay?" he asked.

The Cooper High boy moaned.

Mark shook him a little harder. "Are you okay?"

Barry roared. His right hand snatched. Mark flung himself backward. The clawing fingers missed his face by inches.

Barry screamed, "Kill you!" Despite the airbag, spillage from a bloody nose spotted his face. He tore at his seat belt and airbag, without effect. His thrashing rocked the car.

"Stop!" Mark cried. "You could be hurt, and moving could make it worse!" A wry voice in his mind said, no such luck. The Red Chessman was fit, berserk, and eager to kill him. Mark wished he still had the revolver, but at some point, it had flown from his hand.

Barry's hands began to twitch and pulse. He grunted as if in pain.

"There's no reason to kill me," Mark pleaded. "I'm not your enemy. I brought you here to help you!"

Barry ripped at his restraints. The airbag and safety belt flew to pieces. He scrambled out of the car, jumped up, and came at Mark. His hands were big and grayish now, with inch-long, pointed claws.

Mark bolted. The Red Chessman pounded after him.

The cadet's goal hadn't changed. He still wanted to lead Barry to the cave, where, he prayed, Laurie's influence would calm him, and the sight of Wes's and Traci's bodies would break the spirit's hold over him. But now he was horribly afraid that his pursuer would drag him down before they got there.

But he won't, Mark insisted to himself. I'm light. I'm fast. I've been outrunning mooses like Barry all my life. All I have to do is push.

So he did. His heart pounded. Behind him, footsteps hammered, never flagging.

After a while, Mark realized that nothing looked

familiar. Riding in the car, he'd been coming at the spirit's lair from a different direction, but it still seemed like he ought to have glimpsed the yellow stone or a twisted tree by now. Maybe he was lost.

He did his best to ignore the possibility.

By now, he was gasping. The noise masked the sounds of pursuit. He didn't realize Barry was gaining on him till a hand clutched at his shoulder.

The cadet plunged forward. Barry's fingers missed their hold, but their talons sliced his shirt and skin.

I'm not going to make it, thought Mark. Not unless I slow him down.

Peering ahead through his sweat-smeared glasses, he saw a fallen branch. He stooped, grabbed it, and whirled, swinging the stick in a low arc.

The branch cracked against Barry's knee and broke. The teenager pitched forward. Mark jumped out of the way and ran on. He heard the Chessman spring up and dash after him.

Which was what he'd expected. The question was, was Barry dashing any slower?

Apparently so, because Mark managed to stay ahead of him for five more grueling minutes, till he topped a rise and spied the fang-like rock. "Laurie!" he shouted, as he staggered down the slope.

He expected her to appear instantly. She didn't. What if the spirit had hurt her, or her injuries had been worse than she thought? What if she was passed out or dead?

Trying to keep his lead, he ran on, giving the boundary marker a wide berth to make sure Barry wouldn't touch it. That was about the only thing he could think of that could make his situation worse.

Just then something slammed into him and hurled him to the ground. Barry scrambled on top of him, claws poised to rake his eyes. Mark made a feeble, fumbling grab at his attacker's wrist, and then a girl screamed, "Stop!"

The two boys looked around. Laurie was limping out of the trees.

"Don't hurt him!" she said.

Barry gaped, clearly shocked at her filthy, battered appearance. "But . . . he hurt you! And they killed Traci!"

"No," Laurie said in a firm, soft voice. "Something else hurt me, and Traci, too. I can prove it if you'll let me."

Barry's expression wavered, bewildered one moment, vicious the next. To Mark, it was like watching two personalities fight for possession of the same body.

At last the sane one won, at least for the moment. "Prove it how?" Barry asked.

"By showing you something," his sister said. She pointed. "It's that way."

Barry climbed off Mark. Wheezing, the cadet got up, too. "I was never so glad to see anybody," he said to Laurie. "What kept you?"

"I had to sit," she said. "And the most comfortable place to do it is over there. How was I supposed to know you were going to need me the second you showed up?"

"Show me the proof," Barry growled. Mark noticed his fingers still had claws.

If the bodies don't convince him, thought the cadet, even Laurie won't be able to stop him from ripping me apart.

They all stumbled through the freakish trees. Twice, Laurie swayed. The second time, Mark started to take her hand, but she shook her head. He realized she was afraid their touching would make Barry angry.

When they reached the cave, Mark pulled aside the brier, then took the penlight out of his pocket. "Be quiet," he whispered.

Barry glared at him. "You first. I don't want you behind me." Mark sighed and slipped inside. Laurie followed. Barry had some trouble, but, grunting, managed to wriggle through.

As they tiptoed down the passage, Mark's skin tingled, anticipating a wash of chill. The spirit's sleeping, he told himself. This time, it has no reason to be awake.

And evidently it didn't, because he and his companions reached the pit safely. He shone the light down. Empty eye sockets stared up. The brass buttons on Wes's uniform jacket glinted dully, as did the silver-and-blue-topaz Hudson class ring on Traci's withered hand.

Barry dropped to his knees. His shoulders shook. Unable to see his face in the dark, Mark wasn't sure how he was reacting until he heard him sob.

"They're both there," Mark whispered. "Barry, do you understand what that means? The vision you guys have been watching is a lie."

"I understand," the Cooper boy said. He felt his fingertips and moaned. "What's happened to me?"

"Something turned you into its puppet," Laurie said. "Look, it's complicated. I'll explain when we're out of here." And as they walked away, she did.

When she finished, Barry raked his fingers

through his tangled mane. Fortunately, his nails had nearly returned to normal. "This is the craziest thing I ever heard. A spirit and a warlock making people fight each other. I don't remember any mind-movie. Well, I sort of do . . ."

"Look," Mark said, "the important thing is this. Your buddies are still crazy, and they're planning to murder cadets. Do you think you can stop them?"

"Maybe," Barry said. He looked at the sun, which was dipping behind the trees. "If we can get back in time. The killing could start right after dark."

"Jeez," said Laurie, "I thought you guys would come back in a car."

Twenty-five

As Barry finished reciting the names of the Red Chessmen into the pay phone, Mark broke the connection. The Cooper High student looked surprised.

"You've been on long enough," Mark said. "The police may have a trace on their phones. Come on." They jogged away from the convenience store and down the dark street.

Laurie had insisted they leave her behind so she wouldn't slow them down. The two boys had reluctantly agreed but had made it back to town too late to catch any of the Red Chessmen at home. So they'd phoned warnings to Hudson Academy and the police.

"I got the feeling nobody believed us," said Barry.

"Me, too," Mark replied. "I realize I'm Cooper Hollow's official maniac, but I thought that after what happened in Bowl-a-rama, and with you backing me up, they'd listen." Frustrated, he kicked a mailbox. The metal clanked. "I guess it didn't help that we couldn't explain *why* a bunch of nice, normal townie kids would want to kill people. Or where it's supposed to happen."

"I wish I knew, but as of this afternoon, we hadn't figured it out. I don't know what being a Chessman was like for you, but Reds don't think like regular people. We didn't plan things far ahead. We just knew that when the time came, something would tell us what to do."

"Yeah," Mark said sourly, "the spirit."

"Even if nobody believes us," the Cooper student said, "won't they do *something?* Just in case?"

"Maybe. But do you think Colonel Green can keep the Gray Chessmen indoors if they decide they want out? He hasn't had any luck so far. And how many cops does this little town have? Not many, not enough to search the whole area fast, and who knows what other calls they're handling tonight. I hate it, but I think it's still up to you and me to keep everybody alive. So think. Where *would* your buddies set up ambushes? What places make sense?"

Barry rubbed his chin. "Well, we'd wait for cadets in places where we expected them to go. We'd stay hidden and we wouldn't want witnesses."

"Everybody hangs out at the Nightmare Club and hikes through the woods to get there."

Barry nodded. "That's what I was thinking, too." They quickened their pace. Mark's weary legs ached. His stomach rumbled.

After a block, Barry said, "I never thanked you for snapping me out of the spirit's spell."

"You're welcome," said Mark. "Look, I'm sorry about Traci. I know you liked her a lot."

"Yeah," Barry said. "Seeing the body was rough. But I guess now I'll finally start to get over her. I know she'd want me to."

A dog yapped from behind a picket fence. A

man yelled for it to shut up. "How many guys do we have to find and unbrainwash, anyway?" asked Mark.

"Since Jim, Jerry, and I are out of action, no more than twelve."

"There's no chance of any new recruits?"

Barry shook his head. "When the first few of us got together, we just sort of knew there could never be more than fifteen — one for each chess piece."

Mark frowned. "There are thirty-two chess pieces in a set, sixteen on each side."

"Well, Jim and Jerry only found fifteen."

As Mark mulled that over, they neared Thirteen Bends. The two-lane highway marked the edge of the town proper; not far beyond it was mostly woods. The cadet remembered Laurie telling him that the twisting road had a bad reputation. Supposedly, it had at least one fatal car crash a year, and people sometimes saw the bloody ghosts of accident victims standing alongside it.

The teenager shivered, then smiled. Why should the story make *him* nervous? Compared to what he was going through, spooks who were content to stand harmlessly around would seem like a treat.

The two boys walked across the street, then down a path into the woods. Away from the lights of the town, the night seemed ten times blacker. Branches rustled softly in the breeze.

Mark's nerves buzzed with tension. He started to feel like he was being watched.

Occasionally, they heard someone approaching, and hid till the other kids went by. The last to pass was a gangly cadet with braces.

Eventually Mark recognized the spot where he'd waited for Laurie. He and Barry were getting close

124

to the Nightmare Club. He wondered if they'd been wrong, if the Red Chessmen were actually lurking someplace else. Then a cry shrilled down the trail.

The teenagers dashed forward. Pulling ahead, Mark scrambled up a rise. When he reached the top, he saw four Red Chessmen struggling with the skinny cadet. Evidently, they hadn't been able to resist attacking him, even though he wasn't one of their special enemies. A knife flashed in the moonlight.

Mark charged down the hill, shoved the kid with the knife, and knocked him down. A Chessman with radiant green eyes snarled and swung a chain. Mark jumped back, but the tip of the weapon clipped his hand. He gasped at the pain.

"It's McIntyre!" someone yelled. Forgetting their original victim, who bolted, the Red Chessmen spread out to encircle Mark. He could tell the evil working inside them had warped all four of their bodies, though some of the deformities were hard to pinpoint in the gloom.

A blade streaked at his face. He dodged, and something smashed into his kidney. His sight blurred, and he fell to his knees.

Then Barry raced down the hill. "Wait!" he cried.

The green-eyed Chessman turned. "You made it!" he said. "Just in time to watch this one croak." He whirled the chain over his head.

Barry grabbed the links. "I said, wait! Don't hurt him."

"What's the matter?" asked the Chessman with the knife. He was hunched and long-armed, perhaps the same apelike figure who'd invaded Bowl-a-rama. "You know what this is about. *Traci.*

125

They've got to pay." The other three growled in agreement.

They aren't going to listen, Mark thought. Though still weak with pain, he tried to stand up and run. But a hand grabbed him and threw him flat on the ground.

"Listen to me for two minutes," Barry said. "I'm one of you. You owe me that much."

The goon with the chain stared at him suspiciously. "One minute," he said at last.

"Fine," Barry said. "First, put your chess pieces on the ground."

"What for?" asked a Chessman clutching a length of pipe.

"Just do it. *Please*. You can pick them up when I'm done."

The Cooper High boys glanced at one another, then set the pieces at their feet.

"Okay," Barry said, "here it is. Mark and I found Traci's body in a cave in the woods. Wes's body is with it. Do you see what that means? He didn't kill her. Something else killed both of them. All the stuff we've been thinking is wrong."

The green-eyed Chessman said, "Maybe Wes murdered her, then killed himself. That happens sometimes."

Barry shook his head. "If you'd seen his body, you wouldn't say that. There were too many big wounds. Nobody could tear himself up that bad."

The fourth Chessman, a little guy in an Einstein sweatshirt, said, "But Hudson's done all kinds of rotten stuff to us."

Mark raised himself to his knees. "And you do things to us. It goes back and forth, getting nastier and nastier. This is our last chance to stop it before something horrible happens."

126

The Chessman with the chain sneered. "You mean, before we get rid of you once and for all."

"Listen to yourself," Barry pleaded. "Is that the *real* you talking? Deep in your heart, do you truly want to murder people? Or is something wrong with you?"

"As far as that goes, look at each other," Mark said. "I know it's hard to see anything but what the craziness wants you to, but *try*. The sickness shows in your faces!"

The Chessmen peered at each other. "I can't see it," the boy in the Einstein shirt said. "But I do sort of *feel* it."

The apelike Chessman muttered, "Every night, I dream of Wes killing Traci. Maybe if I can believe it isn't true, it will go away."

The kid with the pipe stared at it as if he'd never seen it before, shuddered, and threw it down.

I don't believe it, Mark thought. It worked. Then the green-eyed Chessman screamed, "Liars!" and whipped the chain at Mark's head.

Caught by surprise, the cadet barely managed to shield himself with his arms. The chain blasted pain through them, tumbled him onto his side, and rattled into the air for a second blow.

But before it could fall, the attacker's friends dragged him down. "We need something to tie him up," said the little guy.

Barry knelt beside Mark. "Are you okay?"

Mark tried to move his arms. They throbbed, but they worked, so he guessed no bones were broken. "Sure," he groaned. "What's another bruise at this point?"

"I'm sorry. I should have stayed ready to jump anyone who made a move on you. But I thought

127

they were all snapping out of it."

"With a little more time, maybe that guy will, too." Mark climbed painfully to his feet. "We've got four down but eight to go. We need to keep moving."

HOW TO APPLY YOUR TATTOO:
1. Moisten the area you want tattooed with water (not too wet or the ink will smear, not too dry, or it won't stick).
2. Place tattoo face down and press on slightly moistened area for a few seconds.
3. Lift up, and now you are tattooed.
4. Washes off with soap and water.
NOTE: Although the tattoo is printed using safe, non-toxic vegetable FDA regulated colors, they are not recommended for sensitive skin or near eyes or to be taken internally.

HOW TO APPLY YOUR TATTOO:
1. Moisten the area you want tattooed with water (not too wet or the ink will smear, not too dry, or it won't stick).
2. Place tattoo face down and press on slightly moistened area for a few seconds.
3. Lift up, and now you are tattooed.
4. Washes off with soap and water.
NOTE: Although the tattoo is printed using safe, non-toxic vegetable FDA regulated colors, they are not recommended for sensitive skin or near eyes or to be taken internally.

HOW TO APPLY YOUR TATTOO:
1. Moisten the area you want tattooed with water (not too wet or the ink will smear, not too dry, or it won't stick).
2. Place tattoo face down and press on slightly moistened area for a few seconds.
3. Lift up, and now you are tattooed.
4. Washes off with soap and water.
NOTE: Although the tattoo is printed using safe, non-toxic vegetable FDA regulated colors, they are not recommended for sensitive skin or near eyes or to be taken internally.

HOW TO APPLY YOUR TATTOO:
1. Moisten the area you want tattooed with water (not too wet or the ink will smear, not too dry, or it won't stick).
2. Place tattoo face down and press on slightly moistened area for a few seconds.
3. Lift up, and now you are tattooed.
4. Washes off with soap and water.
NOTE: Although the tattoo is printed using safe, non-toxic vegetable FDA regulated colors, they are not recommended for sensitive skin or near eyes or to be taken internally.

HOW TO APPLY YOUR TATTOO:
1. Moisten the area you want tattooed with water (not too wet or the ink will smear, not too dry, or it won't stick).
2. Place tattoo face down and press on slightly moistened area for a few seconds.
3. Lift up, and now you are tattooed.
4. Washes off with soap and water.
NOTE: Although the tattoo is printed using safe, non-toxic vegetable FDA regulated colors, they are not recommended for sensitive skin or near eyes or to be taken internally.

HOW TO APPLY YOUR TATTOO:
1. Moisten the area you want tattooed with water (not too wet or the ink will smear, not too dry, or it won't stick).
2. Place tattoo face down and press on slightly moistened area for a few seconds.
3. Lift up, and now you are tattooed.
4. Washes off with soap and water.
NOTE: Although the tattoo is printed using safe, non-toxic vegetable FDA regulated colors, they are not recommended for sensitive skin or near eyes or to be taken internally.

Twenty-six

The first team of ambushers led Barry and Mark to the next. This time, the cadet hung safely back while Barry and the first squad tried to convince the four members of the second to shake off the spirit's influence. Three were persuaded, and helped restrain the fourth. Then everyone trekked on to confront the last group. After a few minutes of heated argument, those four threw away their chess pieces, too.

By that time, the two kids bound with belts and strips of cloth looked sheepish, not angry. The feverish sheen had left their eyes, and their gnarled bodies had straightened. Mark figured it was probably safe to untie them.

The cadet felt himself relax. He and Barry had gotten to the Red Chessmen before they managed to hurt anybody, and now they were all dehypnotized. At least one of his problems was finally over.

"What do we do now?" Barry asked.

Mark said, "Go to the police."

The Cooper High kids stood silent for a moment. Then Roger said, "Look, if we admit what

129

we did, we're going to be in trouble." He waved his automatic pistol as if to emphasize just how much trouble that could be.

Mark said, "The cadets you've been feuding with are still crazy. *They* want to kill *you,* and we need to get them back to normal before they can. If we *all* tell the cops what's been happening, they'll have to believe us, and help us."

Roger frowned. "Okay. I guess it is the only smart thing to do. But my mom and dad are going to kill me."

"I just wish I *understood* what happened," said a kid in a nylon windbreaker. "*Why* did we all go nuts? I mean, Traci was nice, but I didn't even know her that well."

Barry said. "It's weird. So weird—" He fell on his face.

For an instant, Mark thought he'd tripped. Then something popped. As he pivoted toward the noise, a ragged volley of pops sounded, and lights flashed among the trees. Two Cooper students dropped.

Mark realized that the Gray Chessmen had crept up on them and started shooting, no doubt with rifles stolen from the academy. Perhaps Greg's magic had guided them to their rivals.

The Red Chessmen started to run. Mark stooped and strained to pick up Barry. The larger boy lolled, dead weight. In the darkness, Mark couldn't tell where the wound was, or even if he was still alive.

"Somebody help me!" Mark screamed. "Somebody help everybody!"

Roger wheeled, ran back, and grabbed one of Barry's arms. Other Cooper kids hoisted their fallen friends and staggered forward.

The gunfire banged on. Mark felt shots ripping through the air around him. Two more boys fell. One started screaming.

Barry's weight ground pain through Mark's bruised, exhausted body. Got to keep going, he told himself. Get out of the woods. We'll be safe—

Light flashed ahead. Roger fell, dragging Barry and Mark down with him. The rifle fire crackled.

"My leg," Roger whimpered.

"We're surrounded!" shrilled someone else.

"Group together!" Mark shouted. "Follow my voice!" He looked at Roger. Even in the gloom, he could see that the other teenager's face had turned white. "Can you walk? Help me move Barry?"

"I'll try."

Backs bent, they dragged the unconscious boy to a spot where trees and a dip in the ground provided cover. Roger's breath hissed with every step. Mark yelled, "Here! Here!" Red Chessmen scuttled out of the murk and flung themselves down beside him.

"Where's Jay?" asked a horrified voice.

"What are we going to do?" cried another. A hand clutched Mark's arm.

He turned. Everyone was staring at him. Great, he thought, from social reject to leader in one night. Too bad I'm too scared to enjoy it. Too bad I'm not going to *live* to enjoy it.

Not unless he found a way out. He closed his eyes and tried to think.

"All right," he said after a moment. "We've got what, four pistols?" Someone nodded. "Then we shoot back. We can't beat all those rifles, but maybe we can hold them off till somebody hears the shooting and sends help. Who knows first

131

aid?" Two kids raised their hands. "You help the hurt guys. Somebody else, untie the tied-up guys. The rest of you"—he shrugged—"I don't know, just keep your heads down."

Roger gave his automatic to the kid in the Einstein sweatshirt. The boys with handguns opened fire.

Mark shone his penlight over Barry, searching for his wound. When he saw it, his stomach churned. The unconscious boy's left ear was a gory ruin. He pressed his hand against it, trying to stop the bleeding.

The crossfire whined overhead, thumped into the dirt, and blasted splinters out of tree trunks. The air reeked of burnt gunpowder. Mark's eyes stung.

And soon it became clear that the Cooper High boys' fire wasn't slowing the cadets much. Mere shadows in the darkness, the Gray Chessmen darted forward, from one bit of cover to the next.

"I have a problem," the guy in the Einstein shirt said. "I'm running out of bullets."

"Me, too," another kid replied.

Mark strained, listening for the wail of sirens. So far, there was nothing.

Clutching the wound in his thigh, Roger said, "We aren't going to make it, are we?"

"Maybe not," Mark admitted. And then he had an idea.

"I'm Mark McIntyre!" he bellowed. "You don't want me! Greg told you not to hurt me! And I don't want to hurt you! I just want out of here!" He jumped up and ran.

Guns blazed. He waited for the shots to slam into his body. But if any of the Gray Chessmen had been targeting him, they missed.

He dashed on, past Warren lurking behind a

tree, a lever-action rifle in his hand. The Asian boy sneered, but didn't try to stop him.

Mark ran for another half minute, until he was sure he was out of everyone's sight. Then he turned and slunk back.

As he sighted Warren again, a Cooper boy leaped up and tried to flee. The Asian boy swiveled and fired. The Red Chessman stumbled, then ran on. Warren shot again. This time the Cooper student dropped.

Holding his breath, Mark tiptoed forward. His foot snapped a twig.

Warren whirled. Mark launched himself in a flying tackle, plowed into the other boy and took him down. Clinched, they rolled across the ground.

The rifle's hot muzzle was in front of Mark's face. The gun went off; the bullet streaked by his forehead.

He clawed and battered his opponent, to no avail. Bringing his unnatural strength to bear, Warren started forcing the rifle into line to shoot him.

Mark snapped his head forward and butted him. Warren yelped and hurled himself backward. Mark scrambled after him, punching. He had to stay on top of the other boy, giving him no room to use the rifle.

He hit Warren in the stomach, then the face. His eyes rolling up, the Asian boy flopped to the ground unconscious.

Mark waited a second, making sure he wasn't going to get up again, then peered around. As far as he could tell, no one else had noticed the scuffle. The night was dark, the battle was noisy, and the Gray Chessmen were too intent on their prey.

The cadets were rapidly closing in for the kill,

133

and, as best he could judge, only two defenders were shooting back.

As Mark picked up Warren's rifle, he realized there was no point in sniping at Gray Chessmen, even if he could bring himself to do it. He couldn't shoot them quickly enough to prevent a massacre. His only hope was to stop this craziness at its source. He crept around the circle of attackers.

He spied a hunched figure, moved close enough to see it was Stan, and sneaked on.

The next shooter wore a cap, bill turned backward. Just as Mark slipped close enough to see that it was Bob, the black teenager turned. Mark flung himself behind a patch of brush. Frowning, his purple eyes glowing, Bob peered about, then turned and resumed shooting.

Mark's heart pounded. His mouth was dry and tasted rusty. He took a deep breath, let it out slowly, and stalked on. A moment later, he spotted a pair of figures behind an oak.

He eased forward. Because the two boys were in shadow, he had to get close before he could see they were Ken and Greg.

Ken was bare-chested, his body so squat it seemed too muscle-bound to move. His rifle was like a toy in his swollen hands. His altered face was so brutish that Mark might not have recognized him, except for the Ross Perot ears.

Greg looked almost as grotesque. His right hand was withered and spotted, his left eye, milky. He smelled like rotten meat. Since he couldn't score points by killing anyone himself, he hadn't bothered to bring a gun. Evidently he was confident that his magic and Ken would keep him safe.

And that, thought Mark, was where he was

wrong. He raised his rifle and aimed at the back of the warlock's head.

The barrel of the gun shook.

Come on! Mark told himself. You *have* to do this. There's no other way. Somehow he steadied his weapon, reaimed, and squeezed the trigger.

The gun clicked. The magazine was empty.

Twenty-seven

Greg and Ken spun. Obviously, they'd heard the hammer fall. The squat cadet pointed his rifle. Mark swallowed and lowered his.

"You tried to kill us," Ken growled.

"No," Mark said. "Only him."

"And after we let you escape, too," Greg said. "You're not a very grateful person, are you?"

Mark looked at Ken. "Listen to me. You're not a murderer. You don't really want to kill those guys. Greg has you hypnotized."

"I don't know what you're talking about," Ken said. "I've always hated the jerks from Cooper High, and I sure want to make this bunch stop hassling us."

"Look at Greg," Mark said. "Check out his eye, and the way his hand twisted up. You can see there's something *wrong* with him."

Ken snorted. "You're crazy."

Greg smiled. "Ken really can't see it, any more than he understands what I'm saying now. He and his friends are completely programmed. Which means they're full of bloodlust. Even if you did manage to murder me, it wouldn't save my patron's dupes. The cadets would kill them anyway."

Mark didn't think that was necessarily true. He had an idea about how to return the Gray Chessmen to normal. But it wasn't likely to do him much good with Ken's rifle trained on him and the warlock still alive.

Sirens wailed nearby, probably on Cross Road or Thirteen Bends. "You hear that?" Mark demanded.

Greg smiled. A web of wrinkles spread from the corner of his filmy eye. "I imagine we still have time to finish our business. And you. After that, if need be, my little army can shoot it out with the police, distracting them while I steal away."

Mark trembled. "Remember, if you kill me, the spirit scores a point."

"So you know that much," said the warlock. "You're right, but alas, your survival was only important when I was worried that the game would be close. Now that I'm about to rout the opposition, one little pawn doesn't matter. And I owe you for stealing my spell book, and generally meddling in my business. Shoot him, Ken."

"No, Ken!" Mark cried. "When the bleachers fell, I saved your life!"

Ken blinked. For a moment, he seemed confused. Then he sneered, and his thick sausage of a finger tightened on the trigger.

Mark threw the empty rifle at Ken and dove.

Ken flinched from the missile. His gun's muzzle jerked as it went off. Pain stabbed into Mark's left shoulder. Oh, God, I'm shot! he thought. But there was no time to think about it now.

Before the Chessman could recover his balance, Mark slammed into him. He knocked him back, snatched up Warren's rifle, and scrambled in pursuit.

Gripping the barrel, he swung at Ken's hand. The blow cracked, and the Chessman squawked. Mark struck again. The rifle flew out of the senior's grasp.

But it didn't fly far enough. If Mark went for it, Ken would be all over him before he picked it up. He was going to have to finish the fight the hard way.

He lunged, clubbing, praying that he could hit hard enough to get through the Chessman's thick layer of muscle. Meanwhile, the senior grabbed at him. Mark ducked and dodged, certain that if Ken ever got his hands on him, he'd tear him apart.

Ken punched at Mark's stomach. The lighter boy twisted aside. Ken's fist only grazed him, but it sent him reeling. The Chessman bellowed and charged.

Mark fought to regain his balance. Somehow he got his feet planted, whirled the gun into the air, and slammed it down. The stock splintered on the senior's beetle-browed coconut of a head. Ken collapsed.

Gasping, Mark pivoted unsteadily toward the loaded rifle. Greg was about to pick it up.

Mark rushed him. He bashed the warlock away, dropped his cracked weapon, and grabbed the other gun himself. As he leveled it, he snarled.

Greg leered, his hair beginning to fall out in clumps.

Mark felt something stir in the air around him. Instinct prompted him to throw the gun. As it flew from his hand, it exploded.

The warlock spat out several teeth. "Give up. You can't hurt me. And the massacre is about to begin in any case."

Mark sprang at him.

Greg swung his shriveled claw. The backhand blow cracked against Mark's forehead. As he fell, he remembered how the warlock had shattered the front of the trophy case with just a tap of his knuckles.

Greg kicked. Mark rolled away and scrambled to his feet. The world tilted, nearly dumping him back on the ground. Whether it was the bullet wound or the knock on the head, something was making him dizzy.

Don't worry about it! he told himself. Just get him! He lunged.

This time he managed to block two punches, hook his leg behind Greg's, and dump him on the ground. He threw himself on top of the warlock and hammered.

He landed good punches. He could tell he was doing damage. But he couldn't knock Greg out. And suddenly the world began to spin. He could feel his strength leaking away. He was terrified he was going to pass out.

He hit Greg twice more, then tore at his left hip pocket. The warlock thrashed.

Cloth ripped. Coins, a comb, and a Bic pen spilled onto the ground. Mark attacked the right-hand pocket. Something inside it chilled his fingers. Greg started struggling even harder.

Just as Mark touched the cold thing, Greg punched his wounded shoulder. The world went gray. Clinging to consciousness by sheer will-power, Mark grabbed the object, flung himself away, and scrambled to his feet.

As he'd hoped, his prize was a gray wooden chess king, a miniature minaret with a Maltese cross on top. When he'd learned that the Red Chessmen had only found fifteen pieces, he'd suspected that both the spirit and Greg had kept one for themselves. He'd already guessed that the kings were the other ends of the strings that helped control the puppets.

Bleeding and completely bald, Greg lurched up. "Give me that!" he croaked.

"Yeah, right," Mark jeered. He gripped the freezing king in his bloody hand. He felt power pulsing in the air around him, just as he had when Greg blew up the gun. "Cadets! Don't hurt anybody! Don't hate the Cooper guys! Be free!"

Greg pressed his hands, both withered now, to his temples. For a moment, Mark sensed the warlock's natural power striving against the magic in the game piece.

And then the shooting stopped. Fearful that Greg would snatch the king away from him and use it to reestablish control, Mark dropped it, ground it against a rock with his foot, and felt it break apart.

"You *wretch!*" Greg said. He pounced.

Mark tried to defend himself, but his strength was gone. Greg threw him down and began to choke him.

Then all of a sudden, Greg's tight grip relaxed. Snarling angrily, the warlock jumped up, and scuttled quickly away.

A flashlight beam swept over Mark. Officer Murphy crouched beside him. The boy tried to tell him to chase the warlock, but he passed out before he could.

Twenty-eight

When Mark awakened, he was amazed at how comfortable he felt. For the first time in days, he felt completely clean, and lay in a warm, soft bed. If not for the ache in his shoulder, he might almost have imagined that all his struggles had been a dream.

All his struggles! What the heck had finally happened? His eyes flew open.

He was in a hospital room. A tube connected a hanging bag of clear fluid to the needle in his right forearm. The sun shone through the venetian blinds, drawing yellow stripes across his blanket. Officer Murphy sat in the corner, reading a thick hardcover book.

He looked up and smiled. "Hello, son. I expect you'd like these." He handed Mark his glasses.

"Yeah," Mark replied, putting them on. "Thanks." He wondered if the policeman was mad at him for escaping. It didn't seem like it. "How's Barry?"

"He's going to lose the hearing in the one ear, but other than that, he'll be okay."

"How's everybody else?"

"Alive."

Mark's body went limp with relief. "I didn't even let myself hope for that. I mean, Cooper kids were getting shot left and right."

"Fortunately, it was with .22 rimfire ammunition. That does less damage than higher caliber or centerfire ammo. Of course, we're pretty darn lucky even so. The other boys tell me that you stopped the fight."

Mark said, "Yeah. But it's going to be hard to explain."

The policeman's mouth twisted. "I'll bet, because nobody else has told me anything that makes sense. A bunch of them claim they're *forgetting* what happened. Others say that you and Barry are the only ones who know the whole story. That boy just came out of surgery. He'll be unconscious for hours yet. So *you* fill me in. Start by telling me where Laurie Frank is."

Horrified, Mark remembered that they'd left her in the woods. Suddenly, a vision popped into his mind. Laurie lay unconscious in a scatter of brown leaves, a pine cone resting near her outflung hand. Dry and fresh blood stained her forehead. Completely shriveled and ancient now, Greg stood over her. He pressed a finger to his liver-colored lips.

Mark knew instinctively that he was seeing something real. "I don't know where she is," he said.

"I think you do," Officer Murphy said. "Two kids are missing, Greg Tobias and Laurie. I'm not too worried about Greg. The other cadets say he was the ringleader who got you in trouble, so I figure he ran away. But as far as I know, Laurie had no reason to do that. Still, her

142

brother was in the Cooper High chess gang, and she turned up at the fight in the bowling alley, so her disappearance must be tied in with this somehow."

Mark shook his head. "I don't know anything about it."

"Then tell me what you do know," the policeman said. "Why did all you kids turn so vicious? Why did both sides carry chess pieces? Where's this cave where you saw Wes Lombard and Traci Elmore's bodies?"

"I want to talk to my parents and a lawyer before I say anything."

"Don't be like that. Even though we know now you didn't kill the goat, or cause all that destruction by yourself, you're still in trouble. If you really saved lives last night, there's a good chance that I can get you out. But only if you cooperate."

"I can't."

Officer Murphy scowled. "I wish I knew what you think you're doing. If that girl comes to harm because you wouldn't help me find her, you're going to pay for it. For now, you're under arrest. For breaking and entering, trespassing, destruction of property, assault, battery, and escape." He read Mark his rights. "Tell the nurses if you decide to talk." He handcuffed the boy's right arm to the bed rail.

After the policeman left, Mark murmured, "All right, I didn't talk. What do you want?"

Again, the vision bloomed inside his head. "I want you," Greg said. "I've worked up some special magic to pay you back for murdering me."

"I didn't," Mark said. "All I did was keep you from killing other people."

143

"Don't be stupid!" the withered creature snarled. "Look at me! Since none of the Cooper High boys died, I didn't *win!* And now my life is leaking away!"

"Talk to the spirit," Mark said. "Since the game was a tie, maybe it'll play you another." Not that he wanted the deadly contest to begin again, but Greg looked furious. Mark would say anything to keep him from hurting Laurie.

Greg shook with anger. "Don't you think I tried that? It refused. It said that controlling slaves at a distance had already weakened it for years to come. It said it needs to hibernate. I think the vile thing just wants to watch me die!

"If I were able, I'd destroy it. As it is, I'll have to settle for you. Come to these woods tonight." Mark realized that the doddering husk might be too feeble to come to him. "Alone. Otherwise, your sweetheart dies."

"How do I know you won't kill her anyway?"

Greg's gray mouth smirked. "I will. But only after she lures you to me. Or at midnight, whichever comes first. If you haven't shown by then, I'll assume you're not coming."

"Can you see me like I see you?" The boy raised his arm and rattled the handcuffs. "I'm a prisoner. I *can't—*"

"Midnight," the warlock said. The vision faded.

Twenty-nine

Mark's pulse raced. He panted. Realizing he was starting to panic, he struggled to stay calm.

It'll be all right, he told himself. I held my own with Greg when he had a bunch of maniacs backing him up, and I can do it now, too.

But only if he could free himself.

He tried to slip the shackle off his bruised, swollen hand. The cuff was too tight. He lubricated it with spit, then tried again. It still wouldn't go.

He looked at the bed rail. He'd need tools to take it apart.

He pushed the call button on the bed frame. After a minute, a heavy, moon-faced man in white came through the door. His dirty-blond mustache needed trimming. It looked like it was growing into his mouth. He had a blue plastic folder under his arm. "What's up?" he asked in a genial voice.

"I need to use the bathroom," said Mark.

The nurse picked up a bedpan from the high, bedside table. "Here you go."

"I'd rather use a regular toilet."

The nurse shook his head. "No can do. Dr. Garrick doesn't want you getting up yet. Besides which, the cops say you're good at escaping, and that it usually involves a trip to the john."

"Okay, give it to me," Mark said glumly. The nurse handed him the pan. "You can come back for it later, okay?"

"Sure," said the man in white. He opened the blue folder, wrote a note, and lumbered out.

Mark set the pan beside him, then closed his eyes and tried to think.

He couldn't slip the cuff off. He didn't have the key. He couldn't con the nurse into freeing him. And he couldn't take the bed apart. What options did that leave?

He could still tell Officer Murphy the truth. Then, assuming the cop believed him, they could confront Greg together. But he was afraid the warlock would know he'd told, and kill Laurie instantly.

Mark could try to overpower the nurse. But the man was big. Mark didn't feel terribly weak, but he was lying in a sickbed with one arm hurt and the other chained. And the adult might not have a handcuff key on him anyway.

Mark's fists clenched in frustration. Then he got an idea.

He pushed the call button. After several minutes, the nurse returned. Fortunately, he'd brought the hospital chart with him. "Should I take the pan now?" he asked.

"Not yet," Mark answered. "I didn't need it after all. But could you get me a drink?" He waved his hand at the pitcher on the table, trying to make the gesture look feeble. "If I try to reach that far, it really hurts."

"Glad to," said the nurse. He set the binder down, filled a paper cup, and passed it.

Mark drank, then dropped the cup on the green-carpeted floor. Praying he'd made it look like an accident, he said, "Sorry."

"No problem," said the nurse, bending over.

The pages in the folder had paper clips stuck on their edges, probably to hold documents until they could be filed properly. Mark pulled one off, closing his fist on it just as the nurse straightened up. "Did you need anything else?" asked the adult.

"Not now."

"Okay. Just buzz when you do." He pushed the table closer, poured another cup, and left.

The teenager straightened the paper clip, bent a hook in the end, and inserted it in the shackle's keyhole. Heroes in movies could pick locks with a scrap of wire. He ought to be able to do the same.

He tried for a long time. Eventually, the bands of light cast by the venetian blinds crept across the bedspread. Mark knew the sun was sinking. This work wasn't as physically hard as the digging he'd done, but it was still difficult. His fingers cramped, and his shoulder ached.

And at least when he'd been digging, it had been obvious that he really was moving dirt. As the hours passed, and the copper wire scraped and clicked endlessly, he couldn't tell if he was ever going to accomplish the task.

The sunlight dimmed. He took the wire out of the lock to reshape the hook, as he'd done at least a dozen times before. His weary fingers quivered. The clip fell, bounced on the edge of the bed, and dropped off.

Mark peered down. The clip must be lying on the carpet, but in the gloom, he couldn't see it.

He lay on his right side and reached his free left arm through the rail. His fingers didn't touch the floor.

He strained, stretching and grinding his shoulder against the barrier. His wound throbbed. He thought of Laurie at the mercy of the grizzled, stinking thing that Greg had become, and strained harder.

His fingertips brushed carpet. He moved them back and forth. Finally! He felt the clip.

He tried to pick it up. For a second, it felt like it was going to pop out of his grasp again, but then he had it.

Holding his breath, he lifted it, put it in his lap, and panted. He felt his shoulder bleeding, and hoped he hadn't torn out all the sutures. When his trembling abated, he flexed his hand, trying to work the soreness out. He finished reshaping the wire, and attacked the lock once more.

He had to stop when the nurse came in, bringing a supper tray and pills. He ate his food, needing the break, but he soon grew impatient as he watched the light outside the window gray and die.

Taking a deep breath, he began to work the lock again. Abruptly the handcuff clicked open.

For a moment, Mark simply stared, almost unable to believe it had finally yielded. Why now? he wondered. What had he just done that was any different from what he'd been doing for the past few hours?

It didn't matter. He stripped the adhesive tape off his forearm, pulled the IV out, threw off his covers, and stood up.

The world spun. He swayed, and clutched at

the bed for balance. For a second, he was afraid he was too weak to walk, but then the dizziness passed.

The next problem was clothes. At the moment, he was wearing a hospital gown, the kind that fastens in the back. He couldn't very well sneak out of the building and across town in that.

He skulked to the closet. His tattered garments were inside. Some kind person had even washed them. He pulled them on.

He emptied the pitcher in the bathroom sink, then used it and the bedpan along with one of the two pillows to form a long shape on his bed. With luck, in the dark, it might look like somebody was still lying there. Once he'd arranged the covers as best he could, he cracked open the door.

There was no guard posted outside. Keeping his head bowed to hide his face, Mark walked down the hall, past other patient rooms where TVs chattered. He had to resist an impulse to run.

He was sure that someone was going to realize who he was, or at least that he wasn't supposed to leave. His bare arms were black with bruises, and the tattered Iron Maiden shirt was conspicuous, too. But no one gave him a second glance.

He slipped past the glass-walled nurses' station, down the service stairs, and out an exit into the cool night air. All right, he thought grimly. Now for the hard part.

Thirty

Once Mark entered the woods, the night seemed almost unnaturally dark. The chill breeze whispered. A heavy stick in his hand and his pockets full of stones, he sneaked forward.

Then something fluttered. The teenager couldn't place the sound. The hairs rose on the back of his neck.

Ahead, glimmering strips ran from one tree to the next. It looked like giant spiders were building webs.

The cadet crept closer. He had to get within fifteen feet before he could see that the strands were lengths of yellow tape with POLICE BARRIER—DO NOT PASS printed on them. They were rustling in the wind.

Now that Mark knew what the noise was, he felt even more uneasy. He'd obviously reached the site of last night's gunfight. Here he'd robbed Greg of his next hundred years of life, and here, he suspected, the warlock would try to take his revenge.

The boy turned. He didn't see anyone. Maybe Greg wasn't here after all. He relaxed slightly. Then the breeze gusted, and brought him a whiff of stink.

Abruptly, he remembered how Greg's magic had hidden the Gray Chessmen in Cooper High. He hurled himself to one side.

Something cold sizzled past him. Greg and Laurie shimmered into view. The warlock seemed shrunken, inches shorter than before. Flaps of blotchy flesh dangled under his jaw. Even in the dimness, his filmy eye shone white. As in the vision, the girl lay motionless at his feet.

Greg waved hands like chicken feet. As the magic seethed by Mark's head, he dodged, then snatched a rock and threw it.

The stone grazed the side of Greg's head and tore his ear off. Black fluid surged from the wound. The warlock yelped.

That's for Barry! Mark thought. He wheeled and ran. The ancient creature shambled after him.

All right, the teenager thought, so far, so good. He'd drawn Greg away from Laurie, and he ought to be able to keep ahead of a two hundred year-old man. He'd turn, hit, and run, turn, hit, and run, striking by surprise till the warlock dropped.

Greg cried words that were all clicks and hisses. A tree swung a limb at Mark.

The blow spiked agony through Mark's wounded shoulder. He dropped to one knee. Making a grinding sound, the tree bent toward him, its branches writhing like tentacles.

Somehow, Mark shook off the pain, leaped up, and dashed on. Leaves swished down his back.

Other trees struck at him. Then something grabbed his ankle, and he fell.

He snatched his foot free just before the root

could clutch it tight. But as he jumped up, a freezing blaze of magic clipped the left side of his body.

He sprawled back on the ground. Aches shot through him. His flesh shriveled, and his sight blurred. Instinctively, he closed his left eye, and found he saw better without it. It had weakened, while the right was as good as before.

Greg cackled. "How do *you* like it? Being *old!*"

For a heartbeat, horror-struck, Mark just wanted to lie there and die. Why not, he was as good as dead already. Even if he could survive with half his body young and the other old, what kind of life would he have? But if he gave up now, the warlock would kill Laurie. So he lurched to his feet.

He hurled another stone. Perhaps because he was throwing one-eyed, it missed. Greg waved his hands. Fearful of losing what vitality he had left, Mark bolted.

Suddenly, running and dodging were almost impossibly hard. His mismatched legs wouldn't work together. No matter how he gasped, he couldn't get enough air, as if his lungs couldn't hold as much as before.

An icy burst of magic knocked him down. His flesh crackled again, but this time the sound seemed fainter. He was going deaf. The sight in his good eye weakened, and his right hand withered till it was almost as misshapen as the left.

That's it, he thought. No more running. If I don't fight now, I won't get another chance. He dragged himself to his knees. Yellow tendrils slithered around him and yanked themselves

152

tight. He realized that he'd fallen near the crime-scene barrier, and the plastic tape, animated by the same magic that had roused the trees, had entangled him.

He thrashed. His decrepit body couldn't break free.

Greg shuffled closer, hands poised to strangle. Mark nearly gagged on the warlock's stench. Despite his cloudy vision, the teenager could see that his attacker's flesh had begun to melt like wax. Maybe the strain of using so much magic was speeding up his death.

But it wasn't happening fast enough to do Mark any good. He tore at his bonds. He thought he felt them begin to break, but not quickly enough.

Greg reached for Mark's throat. Then the warlock's right eye turned as white as his left. Startled, he pawed at his face.

Mark flung himself back and forth. Come on! he thought. It's only stupid plastic!

The tape gave all at once, spilling Mark to the ground. He tried to leap up, lost his balance, and fell back. His heart hammered in his chest, the beat irregular.

It doesn't matter! he told himself. Just get up and cream him! Once again, he struggled to rise. This time, he made it. Tottering forward, he swung his club.

He landed two good blows. Greg's melting flesh splattered. Then the warlock lurched in close and grappled. His black-lipped mouth croaking gibberish, he pummeled and clawed.

Mark's club was useless in a clinch. He dropped it and punched, grimly aware that his wasted muscles couldn't match what remained of his opponent's magical strength.

But they didn't need to. Greg's flesh was molten down to the bone. When Mark ripped at it, it came away in handfuls, until he found himself tearing at a bare skull. The warlock shuddered, and screamed a clogged, bubbling cry. His eyes dissolved into black ooze and ran down his cheeks. Then he went limp.

Mark let him fall, then stumbled backward—far enough away to avoid most of the slime on the ground. He sat down heavily. He had to; his heart was skipping worse than ever.

Please, he prayed, give me another hour, so I can help Laurie. *Then* I'll die.

Die. Though he was sure it would happen soon, a part of him couldn't quite grasp it. Which was probably lucky. Otherwise, he'd feel even more scared than he'd been up to now, instead of just dazed.

At least, he thought, I'm going out a winner. Then wet, bony fingers clamped his knee.

Mark's head jerked around, and Greg's skeletal fist hit him in the face. Though scarcely more than bones now, the warlock remained alive—whether by magic or sheer hate.

He struck Mark again. The cadet's glasses flew off. The skeleton grabbed his neck and choked him.

Mark felt darkness sucking him down, but a surge of anger kept him conscious. The fight wasn't going to end like this! He wouldn't give this filthy thing the satisfaction! He punched at its rotten, gap-toothed grin.

Pain blasted down his arm. He'd broken his hand. But Greg's skull shattered, too. Brains splashed and along with them, the evil magic.

154

The warlock fell, clattering. His bones and the scum that had fallen from them turned to powder. The next gust of wind began to scatter it.

When Mark felt able, he recovered his glasses, and clambered to his feet. His throbbing hand cradled against his chest, he staggered toward Laurie. Sometimes he felt light-headed, and he knew he was close to fainting. But he made it.

The girl still lay where he'd left her. When he knelt and touched her cheek, her skin seemed cold. He peered at her and saw she wasn't breathing.

He wondered if she'd been dead a long time, and Greg had concealed the fact to lure him. But what did that matter? All that mattered was that he'd given his life to save her, and she was gone anyway. He started to cry.

A tear fell on her cheek. She twitched and her eyes fluttered opened. He realized that with his blurry vision, he just hadn't *seen* her breathe.

"What?" she said groggily.

"You're safe now," he said. "Greg's dead. You probably don't recognize me, but I'm Mark."

She squinted. "Why wouldn't I recognize you?"

And abruptly he realized that, while he still felt lousy, he didn't feel as awful as before. His heart had stopped juddering, and it was no longer a struggle just to breathe. He looked at his hands. They were bruised, scratched, and swollen, but they were no longer withered with age.

Evidently, when Greg died, it broke his curse. And so Mark was young again.

155

"I'll tell you later," he said. "Can you walk?"

"I guess. Greg made me walk this far before he zapped me to sleep again."

"Then let's get to the Nightmare Club and have them call an ambulance."

Thirty-one

When Mark awoke, his hand was itching. He tried to scratch it and couldn't. Something cold and hard was in the way.

His eyes fluttered open. He was back in his hospital room. This time, one ankle was shackled to the bed frame, and his hand was in a white plaster cast.

"Good morning," said a cheerful female voice.

Mark looked up to see a woman rising from the chair near his bed. It was Jenny Demos from the Nightmare Club. Clad in faded jeans and a chambray shirt, she stood smiling down at him. "I hope you're hungry, because I brought food. Brownies, chocolate chip and oatmeal raisin cookies, and lemon cake. What would you like?"

"Uh, a brownie, I guess. Please." She opened her picnic hamper. He tried to work his fingers under the cast. It was impossible.

Jenny handed him the chocolate snack. "Thanks," he said. "It's nice to see you. I had no idea you'd come."

"I've got too many customers in here and the detention center," the blond woman said. "I can't

157

abandon you to try to survive on institution food. If you die of malnutrition, the Night Owl will go out of business. Besides, I wanted to sign your cast." She took a purple felt-tipped pen out of her pocket. "May I?"

"Sure."

To his surprise, she didn't write her name. Instead she doodled a design that looked something like one of the drawings in Greg's spell book. As she finished, the itch went away. "I suppose Sam Murphy will want you to make a statement today," she said.

He took a bite of the brownie. "Probably."

"Have you thought about what you're going to say?"

"The truth, I guess."

"It's none of my business, but I'm going to give you some advice anyway. The same advice I gave Barry and Laurie. You see, like Laurie, I believe in the Hollow spook legends. I have a . . . shall we say, *hunch* that some of your experiences have been very strange." Mark opened his mouth to confirm that. "No need to tell me if I'm right, just listen. If the trouble's over, and the responsible parties have died, become inactive, or whatever, you might want to consider keeping the weirder details to yourself. Particularly if you don't have any proof."

"I am worried that the police won't believe us, even now," Mark admitted. "I'm sick of people thinking I'm crazy. But I'm also worried about telling a story that's full of holes. The police might get angry. And that won't help get me out of trouble, either."

"I understand. But remember, you've got some nasty bruises on your forehead," noted Jenny. "It

158

wouldn't be too amazing if *your* memory clouded up, too. Along with Barry's and Laurie's." Suddenly, Jenny lifted her head as if she'd heard something. "Excuse me." She disappeared into the hall.

A moment later, Mark heard her say, "Hi, Sam."

"Hi," Officer Murphy's voice answered glumly.

"Why the sour face?"

"I'm frustrated. None of these kids' stories makes any sense."

"Shame on you," she said teasingly. "A detective ought to enjoy a good mystery."

"Only if he can solve it. Otherwise, it's a royal pain."

"But this time, maybe there is no explanation. Sometimes, groups of people go crazy together. No one knows why, but it happens. Look at the dancing manias in the Middle Ages."

"Right, and the flagellants. But I'm a cop. I'm supposed to build cases against suspects. I can't just say the town had an outbreak of mass hysteria and let it go at that."

"Does that mean these boys are going to be prosecuted?" asked Jenny.

"That's for the District Attorney to decide. But we've got kids laid up with gunshot wounds, and thousands of dollars worth of property damage to boot. So probably."

"Well, the trials ought to be a real circus. I mean, the defendants are also the victims and witnesses, and they don't want to testify against one another. Unless you turn up a lot more information, the prosecution won't even be able to provide a coherent account of what happened. And since Greg Tobias is still missing, you can't

159

produce the most important figure in the case. Or even explain who he really was, if it's true that the parents listed in his Hudson records don't exist."

"How did you know that?" Officer Murphy asked.

"I heard it somewhere. Maybe one of the academy staff told someone else."

"Well, you are right, it's going to be a major hassle to take this in front of a judge—"

"Then don't," Jenny said. "Work out some kind of probation, or just drop the charges. These are good kids, Sam. And they're okay now. I can tell. Don't wreck their lives."

"You know I'd *like* to give them a break—"

"So go for it, and I'll make you dinner. In case I never mentioned it, I went to cooking school in Paris."

He snorted. "Don't you know it's against the law to bribe a cop? Look, no promises, but after I finish my interviews, I'll talk to the DA, and we'll see."

"Thank you," Jenny said. "I need to get moving. I'll see you." Mark heard her move on down the corridor.

The policeman walked into the room, a yellow legal pad in hand. "Hi," he said. "How are you doing?"

"Okay," Mark said.

"Feel any more talkative today? Or do you still want Perry Mason?"

"I'll tell you everything I remember."

As Jenny had suggested, he edited the weirdest parts out, though he did reveal where Wes and Traci's bodies were. He figured that since the cops would go there by day, they'd be safe, particularly if the spirit was hibernating.

Officer Murphy glowered through the recital. At the end, he said, "I know some of that was a lie. I just wish I knew why. But I guess the important thing is that you stopped the shooting, and you brought that girl home. I have to go talk to some people. I'll see you later." He strode out.

Four hours later, he came back and removed the shackle. "Does this mean I'm not under arrest anymore?" asked Mark.

"Yes," the policeman said. "There is no justice." He grinned. "Well, maybe there is. Take care of yourself. Stay out of trouble."

"Don't worry," Mark said. "I've had enough to last me."

For a while, Mark was content to lie and bask in the knowledge that his problems were finally over. But soon, he started getting bored. His room didn't even have a TV. He figured he'd have to rent one, like his mom had when she'd been in the hospital before.

Well, he wasn't chained up anymore. And though his doctor might want him to stay in bed, no one had *told* him to. At least, not today. He got up.

For a moment, he felt lightheaded, but then it was all right. Stiff, bruises twinging, he hobbled down the hall.

A few doors down, he found a patients' lounge. Several kids sat around the TV, ragging on *General Hospital*. With their bandaged heads, Laurie, Barry, and Ken looked like mummies. Roger was still wearing his skull earring; a pair of crutches lay at his feet. Another Cooper High boy had one arm in a sling and tape across his nose.

When they noticed Mark, they all babbled greetings and questions, grinning like idiots the whole time. Then a hand fell on his shoulder.

He turned. His parents stood in the doorway, red-eyed and disheveled.

Mark had to stifle a laugh. He was glad to see them, but it was funny that they'd raced all the way from South America, only to get here after everything was over.

They obviously didn't share his amusement. When they saw how chewed-up he looked, their mouths fell open. His mom sobbed and flung her arms around him.

"I'm okay!" he said. At least he would have been, if the hug weren't mashing his shoulder.

"You *will* be," his father said grimly. "I promise. I don't know what's been going on here, but I know my son is no criminal. I'm going to hire the best lawyer in New York."

"You don't need to," Mark said, squirming free of his mother's embrace. "You're behind on the news. The police let us go."

Dad blinked. "Oh. Well. Then as soon as the doctor says you can leave, we'll get you out of here. Del Hicks's boy goes to a school in Kentucky—"

Mark's eyes widened in alarm. "Won't Hudson take me back?"

Dad frowned. "Well . . . yes, actually. Colonel Green said that all of you who got in trouble could come back on a trial basis, once your legal situations were resolved. I guess he can't afford to lose fifteen cadets in one fell swoop."

"But you can't stay *here!*" Mark's mother said. "You never had any trouble anywhere else. Now you've been arrested, beaten and shot by psychotic—"

"I'm staying," Mark said firmly. "I've finally found a school where I feel at home." He smiled at the other injured kids. "What can I tell you, these psychos are my friends."

About the Author

RICHARD LEE BYERS is a talented and acclaimed author who holds a B.A. and an M.A. in Psychology. Before becoming a writer, he worked as a psychotherapist and administrator in the mental health field.

When Richard was growing up in Columbus, Ohio, he enjoyed reading classic novels in the genre of the fantastic including H.G. Wells' books *The Time Machine, The War of the Worlds,* and *The Invisible Man,* and Edgar Rice Burroughs' *Tarzan* and *Mars* books. Those works greatly influenced Richard as a writer, as well as books by authors Fritz Leiber, Robert E. Howard, and H.P. Lovecraft.

Richard now resides in the Tampa Bay, Florida area. His recent adult novels include *The Vampire's Apprentice* and *Dead Time.* His short stories have appeared in *Freak Show, Grails: Quests, Visitations, and Other Occurrences, Confederacy of the Dead,* the *Tampa Tribune, 2AM, New Blood, Eldritch Tales, Amazing Experiences,* and *Quick Chills: The Year's Best Horror from the Small Press, Volume One.*

Richard likes to hear from readers. He, and

everyone at *The Nightmare Club*, would enjoy hearing how you like the books, and what you'd like to see in future stories. Write to him, c/o The Nightmare Club, Zebra Books, 475 Park Avenue South, New York, NY, 10016. If you'd like a reply, please include a stamped, self-addressed envelope.

SNEAK PREVIEW!
Here is a special preview of the next
Nightmare Club.
The Mask by Nick Baron will be available in
September 1993.

The Nightmare Club #4
THE MASK
by Nick Baron

Sheila Holland felt the soft caress of sunlight as it broke through the steel gray clouds through the window, to touch the side of her face. Sitting at her desk in fifth period Natural Studies, she closed her eyes and pretended that the sunshine was the strong, warm hand of Ian Montgomery touching her. Pretending was all she could do. Ian didn't know she was alive, and probably never would.

The light faded. Sheila opened her eyes and shifted her gaze to the clock on the other side of the classroom. Eleven fifty-five. Ten more minutes and Mrs. Lang's class would be over. Twenty-five of her classmates surrounded her. Sheila knew the names of each student. She had been to school with many of them since childhood. Their names were the most intimate detail any of them had personally revealed to her in all the years she had known them. It had been long before this, her junior year, that Sheila had given up on learning anything but second hand knowledge of her schoolmates. She was different from them and they would never let her forget it.

Her teacher, a startlingly attractive raven-haired woman stood at the front of the class, delivering a lecture. Sheila liked Mrs. Lang. When she first saw the woman, she had been prepared to hate her. Erika Lang was five-foot-six, trim, soft, and beautiful. Her features were dark and mysterious, sensuous and piercing. The woman's midnight hair spilled onto milk white shoulders that led to a magnificent, hour glass figure and long, perfect legs.

Sheila knew that she possessed no such attributes. She wasn't deformed or anything, she was simply *underdeveloped*. Or so she felt whenever she looked in the mirror. Sheila was five-foot-one, in shape, but lacking any real figure, and cursed to look like a thirteen year-old even though she was now a junior in high school. She had brown, wavy hair that dropped to her narrow shoulders with bangs in the front; sad, brown, milk carton kid's eyes; and a nose that was a little too round and wide for her narrow, oval face and thin lips. She hid her slightly large ears under her hair whenever possible. Today, she wore jeans, a sweater, and a silver love bracelet one of her second cousins gave her as a sort of joke. But she treasured the item because she was the only one who knew that it had not come from her imaginary "out-of-town boyfriend." Sheila had never had a boyfriend. Lots of male friends, but no one that interested her romantically.

No one, that is, except Ian Montgomery, Cooper Hollow's answer to Tom Cruise. Sheila was about to drop back into another fantasy about the life she would have if Ian cared for her when she suddenly heard Mrs. Lang calling her name. She looked up abruptly and knew her expression was that of a deer caught in the headlights. The other students exploded in laughter.

"Sheila, so good of you to join us," Mrs. Lang teased.

She smiled weakly. "Sorry."

In the back of the classroom, a student made a crack. "Yeah, we are, too," it sounded like. Followed by more snickering and laughter.

"We're talking about political repression. Countries suppressing the rights of their people and denying them simple human dignities. Prisoners of conscience. Men and women beaten, tortured, starved, even killed due to their beliefs. I thought you might have something to add."

"Here comes Ms. Brainiac," someone else whispered. "Computing, computing . . ."

More laughter, only a bit restrained.

Fear twisted and gnashed within her guts. She felt as if she had swallowed a clawed serpent. "Sounds like a typical day at Cooper High."

That met with more laughter, but this time, it was the right kind. The kids were laughing *with* her, not *at* her. Sheila knew it wouldn't last. Nevertheless, she smiled nervously and sank a little in her chair, enjoying the moment. Mrs. Lang exhaled a ragged breath, obviously disappointed, and turned sharply to call upon another student.

As class wore on, Sheila found that she had mixed feelings about the remark she had made. No further derisive comments were launched in her direction, and for that, she was grateful. But Mrs. Lang gave her several sidelong glances that told Sheila the woman was less than pleased.

Finally, the bell rang. Sheila had gathered up her books and was ready to bolt for the rear exit when her teacher called to her.

"I'd like to see you for a moment, please," Mrs. Lang said.

The laughter returned. *Ooohs* and *ahhhs*. *The brain is gonna get hers*. That *would be a first*.

The classroom cleared quickly. Sheila made one more attempt to escape, "I'm gonna be late for class."

"This'll only take a minute. I'll give you a pass."

Sheila hung her shoulders in defeat, picked up her books, and walked to Mrs. Lang's desk. Her teacher had worn a white silk top and a black skirt. The skirt ended just before the knees and had a small slit on the side. The woman sat on the edge of the desk, her long, perfect legs dangling. She wore black shoes with only a low heel, and her magnificent legs were gripped by black stockings.

Sheila would have killed to look like this woman. She wondered if Mrs. Lang was even half-aware of the effect she had on the teenaged boys she taught. Sheila heard the boys at lunch, in the halls, at the Night Owl Club. Their comments were sometimes crude, sometimes dreamy, but always attentive. Sheila would have killed for that kind of notice. Instead, she was just a brainy little geek who looked more like a thirteen year-old boy than a knockout like Mrs. Lang.

"What happened?" Mrs. Lang asked.

"I don't know."

"Is it my imagination or did we have an hour long talk after school on Monday about both of us being members of Freedom International and what the organization meant to us?"

"No," Sheila said, suddenly ashamed. "You didn't imagine it."

"Were you nervous?"

Sheila bit her lip. That explanation was as good a way out as any, but she didn't want to lie. "No, I wasn't."

"This could have been a real opportunity for you to show what you've learned."

"You did a good enough job. You didn't need me."

"I can hand out the facts. But I know from talking to you the other day that Freedom International and all they're trying to accomplish is very important to you. You said it yourself, the organization needs the support of younger members. Reaching kids whose views are still forming is best accomplished by the testimony of other kids, not speeches made by adults."

Sheila became angry. "I do my part, all right?"

"Yes," Mrs. Lang said, her voice, impossibly, becoming softer and even more compassionate. "Of course. I wasn't trying to beat up on you. I just want to understand. Are you worried about others knowing that you're in Freedom?"

"No."

Mrs. Lang shook her head. "It seems like you're ashamed of your intelligence and your knowledge. You shouldn't be. Those assets are so important—"

"Didn't you hear what they were saying? I'm the geek, I'm the brain. I have all the answers. I'm not like them."

"And you want to be?"

Sheila bit her lip. She looked back to the doorway to make sure no one had appeared there. In a small, strangled voice she said, "You don't know

171

what it's like. Just once I'd like to be asked out on a date or invited to a party. Just once. They're doing a three night masquerade at the Night Owl Club. It starts tonight, it ends Friday. Halloween."

Mrs. Lang's face lit up. "That's *wonderful*. I'm sure if you go you'll have a wonderful time."

"Yeah, right. I'm just going to show up there? Alone? No one's invited me. As long as people see me as this geeky brain and nothing else, I don't have a chance."

"You can't worry about what other people think about you," Mrs. Lang said. "Sheila, you're going to look back on these years and realize ultimately that what matters is how you see yourself. Be true to yourself."

"That's easy for you to say. You're pretty."

"You're pretty, too, Sheila."

"Then why am I always alone?" Sheila asked as she turned and ran from the classroom.

Mrs. Lang hung her head in defeat. She had no answers.

Ian Montgomery, number seventy-one, commanded the football field. When he was loosed, he was like a Juggernaut—no one could stop him. The few that managed to lay hands on him were soon face down on the ground. The rest found themselves gripping thin air as he raced across the playing field with animal grace and cunning, leaving his competition hopelessly outclassed.

Sheila's camera followed his every movement. Her lens was trained on him with the unerring precision of an assassin's crosshairs. The feelings he elicited within her, however, were anything but cool and detached. He was magnificent. In all her life, she had never seen anything quite like him. She never missed seeing him play, even when, like today, it was only an afterschool practice session.

A nightmarish shape suddenly crowded into her line of vision. Sheila saw crossed hazel eyes, dark unkempt hair, and a squashed button nose. She might have been looking at the creature captured in her viewfinder through a fishbowl. The girl staring into her camera pulled back her lips to make herself look bucktoothed.

"I said, communist pinko marshmallow eaters from the Gamma Quadrant just took over the White House. They've held their first news conference. In it, they stated that by the time Sheila Holland is twenty-five, her boobs will be somewhere around her ankles."

"Thirty," Sheila said, easing her camera from her face and staring into the sardonic visage of her best friend, Gwen Turko. Gwen was a junior, like Sheila, and she dressed in blue jeans, a denim jacket, and a Mickey Mouse tee-shirt pulled down over her waist. Her sunglasses were jammed high into the curly mass that constituted her hair. She had never grown out of the tomboy stage.

"Huh?"

"I've seen pictures of my mom. I'd give it 'til I'm thirty, then it all goes to hell. If I *had* any boobs, that is. Which I don't."

"It's nice to know you're paying attention," Gwen said in her customary sarcastic manner.

They stood on a set of bleachers far enough from the coach and the other players to ensure their comfort and privacy, but close enough to the field to get fantastic shots. Sheila and Gwen were members of the photography club and Nikons hung from both their necks.

173

"What were you, off in the Monkey-Boy Vortex again?" Gwen asked.

"Monkey-Boy" was Gwen's term for Ian. Sheila didn't like it much, but she said nothing. Gwen had admitted that she couldn't understand Sheila's continuing obsession with Ian. She had never been out on a date and had no interest in having a boyfriend. The concept of loving someone the way Sheila loved Ian—even though he didn't know it—was alien to her.

" 'Fraid so."

On the playing field, the coach called for the athletes to huddle. The animal ferocity drained out of Ian Montgomery. He walked back to the coach with an ease and confidence that allowed his movements to be categorized just this side of a strut. Several onlookers called his number. He looked up at them, smiled, and waived.

"Turbo!" one of the players shouted. "When are you gonna get a man!?"

"Why? You know where I can find one, meatball?" Gwen shouted in return. When she spoke again, it was only to Sheila. "Mark again. God, I really want to kick his butt."

Sheila nodded. Gwen's last name was Turko, but her friends and detractors alike sometimes called her Turbo, instead. She was always on about something, ready to go into battle for any cause. If none existed, she was prepared to make one up.

Her relatives, teachers, and family physician warned that she would suffer either a heart attack, an ulcer, a cerebral hemorrhage, or all of them if she didn't slow down. Gwen told them to take a pill and relax. She'd live to be one hundred and six and dance on their graves.

Her penchant for gruesome statements like that

had led her—at her parents' insistence—into one long conference with the school psychiatrist. The result had been that the doctor and Gwen had traded useless facts about horror movies. The psychiatrist, named Carry White, had grown up sharing a name with one of Stephen King's most popular creations. Her sympathies were with Gwen.

In the most polite, scholarly terms, Dr. White told Gwen's parents to take a pill. Their daughter would easily live to be one hundred and six and would, most assuredly, take great delight in dancing on a *lot* of people's graves. She was too healthy, both in mind and body, and too ornery, for any other fate.

On the field, Mark Phillips, player sixty-nine, made a kissy-motion to Gwen and went to the huddle with his buddies. His walk could *only* be catalogued as a strut.

A few weeks ago, at another practice, Mark had aimed his butt at the girls and told them to get a real good shot. Gwen was obliging. A friend of hers on the school newspaper had been all set to run the shot with the byline, "Mark Phillips Displays His Private Assets." The faculty advisor, a close friend of the coach, pulled it. Sheila's photos occasionally made the newspaper. Not coincidentally, they were always of Ian.

"Have you ever wondered what it would be like to be down there?" Sheila asked, her gaze drifting to the players who were conversing with their coach as several cheerleader types looked on. "Wouldn't it be nice, just once, to be on the inside, looking out, instead of the other way around?"

"Don't be a *pod*," Sheila said, referring to the

aliens who replicated the forms and took over the lives of their victims in the film, "Invasion of the Body Snatchers."

"I'm not a pod," Sheila said with a touch of resentment.

Gwen shook her head. "Sure, I've wondered. I've also wondered what it would be like to be awake and without an anesthetic during open heart surgery. Doesn't mean I want to experience it."

Sheila felt her anger rise. "Don't you take anything seriously?"

"Okay, I'll tell you exactly what it would be like." Suddenly, Gwen assumed an exaggerated upper New York preppy overbite and said, " 'Hi, Buffy.'

" 'Oh, hi, Biff.'

" 'How was football practice?'

" 'Oh, fine, but would you *please* be careful about how much starch you put in my shorts? They seem to be riding up at the most inopportune times.'

" 'Yes, dear. Of course, dear. Anything you *say,* dear. Oh, darling, would you like me to lay down so you can walk all over me with your cleats on?'

" 'Oh, would you? Please, please!' "

"Thanks a lot," Sheila said coldly. She had spent the last half hour before Gwen's arrival fantasizing about what life would be like if Ian Montgomery loved her. The last thing she needed was having her secret dream ridiculed.

"Hey, I was just kidding," Gwen said, her tone softening uncharacteristically. Sheila's stonelike expression did not change. "I was just *kidding,* lighten up."

"Okay," Sheila said impassively. "Whatever."

"You know how I feel about those people—"

"I know. You hate them, they hate you. You're even."

Gwen was surprised by the sharpness of her friend's tone. "I'm not saying you're wrong, but you can really be pretty cold sometimes, you know?"

"She's got it bad, what do you want?" a boy said from somewhere close. The sound of his voice made both girls jump. They turned and saw Jack Kidder standing behind them.

Jack had climbed onto the bleachers behind them without making a sound. He was tall and skinny, with a long, thin face, wild eyes, and a scarecrow's uneven smile. His dark hair constantly flopped into his eyes. Using his elongated, pianist's hands, Jack brushed it away. He wore an army jacket that once belonged to his dad, who was now in prison. A backpack was slung over his shoulders.

"Don't do that," Gwen and Sheila said in unison.

"Do what?" Jack asked as he stepped down to their row and seated himself between them.

"Sneak up on us like that," Gwen said as she slugged him in the arm hard enough to make him yelp with pain. The camera he wore around his neck slapped against his chest.

"All right, all right," he said. Then he gave Sheila a goofy grin. "I guess that's the most physical contact I can expect from my little love poodle today."

"I guess so."

Gwen growled. Jack was always calling her ridiculous pet names. "I'd hit you again, but I'm worried you might like it too much."

177

"Only one way to find out."

Gwen slammed him in the same spot. From his cry of pain and surprise, he evidently did not like it at all.

Rubbing his sore arm, Jack said, "I've got everything cleared for us at the Wakefield Mall."

Her eyes flashing open wide, Gwen said, "You're kidding, right?"

Jack shook his head.

"That's great," Sheila said distractedly. Ian was taking the field once again and she raised her camera to follow his movements.

"The Wakefield Mall," Gwen said, still not quite believing it. "All right!"

Jack sprang out of the way before Gwen could hit him again. "You really need to learn some other way of expressing yourself."

Gwen shrugged.

"I thought they were worried about the controversy," Sheila said as she watched Ian intently and snapped another photo of him.

"New guy took over. He's a member of Freedom International, too. He said we can set up a booth there and distribute flyers all we want. Just try to be cool about it. Don't wrestle anyone to the ground to get them to listen, and be polite if we get any real jerks."

"All right," Gwen said again. Wakefield was in the next county, but the large two story mall was always crowded.

Jack pulled a sketchbook from his backpack and flipped it open to a certain page. "I thought we could go with 'Wake up, Wakefield!' as our slogan. I printed this out on the Laserjet in the computer room. What do you think?"

Gwen nodded. Sheila was lost in the viewfinder

once more. Gwen tapped Sheila's butt with the tip of her sneaker. Spinning around, startled, Sheila quickly realized what was going on and said the slogan looked great. "Very attention-getting."

Jack nodded. "People are dying, people are having their civil liberties denied to them, we've got to do our part."

"Absolutely—" Sheila began. Someone cried touchdown and she whirled back to the playing field and cursed. Ian had scored a goal and she had missed it.

"They want us there on Thursday to set up," Jack said. "Does that work for you two?"

"Yeah," Gwen said.

Sheila felt embarrassed at paying so little attention to her friends. This was a lot more important than staring at Ian, she told herself. Now, if only she could bring herself to believe that. "Absolutely."

"You're not going to run off to the masquerade, are you?" Jack said, teasing.

Sheila sighed. I wish, she wanted to say, but she kept her mouth shut. Ian would be there. Her thoughts suddenly snapped back to the weekend. She had gone to an antique barn with her mother on Sunday. They had spent nearly an hour without finding anything before Sheila came upon the mask.

It was the most beautiful thing she had ever seen, other than Ian Montgomery. She took one look at it and knew she had to own it, even though she would probably have no real use for it. Under other circumstances, her mother might have objected to her throwing away her meager allowance on such an extravagance, but Colleen Holland had other things on her mind. She and

Sheila's dad, Gary, had gone through another of their knock down fights, and Colleen had simply wanted to be out of the house.

Fantasies of going to the masquerade and approaching Ian wearing the mask flashed into Sheila's mind. Maybe she could trick him into loving her. He could get to know her with the mask on, and she would be beautiful because of it, then—

Stupid, she chided herself. Stupid, stupid, stupid. No mask could give her what she needed to compete with the senior girls and the cheerleaders. She would need a miracle for that.

"The only possible conflict I can see is the deadline for the photography contest," Jack said as he tapped his camera. "They want all the entries in by Monday."

Sheila nodded. The Cooper Hollow *Gazette* sponsored the contest every six months. The winner's work was displayed in a gallery downtown and published in the paper's weekend edition.

Jack checked his watch. "I gotta go. Melissa's meeting me at four."

Gwen raised one eyebrow. "Melissa Antonelli?"

"Uh-huh."

Melissa was one of the prettiest girls in the senior class. Jack had suffered a crush on her for years.

Gwen knocked lightly on the side of Jack's head. "Hey! Hey, you! Anyone in there? Don't you remember the last time you shot your mouth off that someone like her was dating you? Her boyfriend beat the hell out of you."

Jack shook his head. "I didn't say we were going out. She's modeling for me. We're going down to the graveyard. There's some really great photo ops there. I figure I'll do some grainy black and white double exposures. She's going to wear this old frilly dress that belonged to her great, great grandmother or something like that. It'll be fun."

Sheila understood now. Melissa wanted to be a model one day. Posing for Jack would give her something to show the agencies. She hoped Jack would realize that's all that it was and not get his hopes up. Melissa usually hung around with creeps like Mark Phillips, not decent guys like Jack.

From Jack's goofy, glazed expression, she could tell that he had concocted an entire scenario in his head. If she called him on it, he would just get defensive.

"Who knows, maybe I'll even get some good portfolio stuff out of it. Something to show Cooper Union, or Visual Arts."

Sheila smiled. Jack wanted to be a professional photographer in the worst way.

"Let's meet at lunch tomorrow and we'll set everything up for Wakefield," he said excitedly.

"Sounds good, Jack," Sheila said, wanting desperately to say something to him, knowing the whole time that it would cause more harm than good. He packed up and ran off.

"She's going to break his heart," Sheila said.

Gwen nodded slowly. "If she does, I'll kill her."

"I'll help."

This time, they both attempted to lose themselves in the practice. Suddenly, Gwen asked, "You're really thinking of going tonight, aren't you?"

"What do you mean?"

"The masquerade."

"I dunno."

"I'll go with you, if you want."

"I don't think either of us would really fit in there, do you?"

"Hey, I'll go anywhere I like. No one's going to tell me where I can and can't go."

"No, they don't *tell* you, they just make sure you wish you were anywhere else, that's all."

"You're right, who needs them, anyway?"

I do, Sheila thought as she watched Ian on the playing field. More than I could ever tell you.

They watched the rest of the practice in silence.

Two weeks earlier, in Mrs. Lang's class, Sheila had seen a reference to Dante's *Inferno*. She found the text in the local library and flipped through the illustrations of the various levels of hell envisioned by the artist. Sitting in silence at the dinner table with her mother and father as they glared at one another, Sheila started to wonder if there had been a few levels that Dante had left out. If so, living with angry parents had to be one of them.

For days, Sheila had wished that her parents would stop arguing. Now that they had, the brooding silence that had taken the place of the shouting and fiery accusations was even more difficult to handle. Dinner had consisted of leftover chicken cooked barbecue style, frozen vegetables, and a tossed salad. The lettuce leaves were turning brown. Sheila considered mentioning this to her mother, but one ice cold glance from the woman was enough to tell her to keep her mouth shut. She helped set the table, mentioned the awareness booster she would be participating in for Freedom International over the weekend, and generally did her best to avoid any subjects that might set the woman off.

She was lucky in one aspect. Her mom and dad did not take their anger out on her, like Gwen's parents. Gwen's mother found fault with everything she did, and the woman had an unnerving habit of stopping Gwen as she went out the door to tell her that they had to "have a discussion" that night. Gwen said it didn't bother her, but Sheila could see the tension mount in her friend as the day went on.

At night, after Gwen's stomach was in knots as she prepared for a battle over some infinitesimal infraction that she had committed against her mother's fluctuating set of rules to live by, the "discussion" would only be a letter that had come for her. Something innocuous like that. When real trouble was on the way, Gwen would get no warning. One minute, everything would be fine, the next, she was the daughter who had let her parents down; a terrible child, a mistake, a willful, ungrateful little brat who didn't deserve anything her parents had slaved to give her.

Sheila had been waiting for the day to arrive when her mother and father started doing the same thing to her, but, so far, she had been spared that kind of abuse.

I'm dancing as fast as I can, Lord, Sheila thought as they said grace. *I'm dancing as fast as I can.*

Dinner went on, with one light moment as Colleen talked about a scene in a sitcom from the other night. The laughter faded quickly, the tension quickly reasserting itself.

Colleen was forty-one, and the years had taken their toll on her youthful beauty. Crow's feet gathered in the corners of her eyes, deep smile lines marked her face, and the muscles of her neck had

183

turned wiry. Her skin, once luminous if photographs were to be believed, was dried out. She had dark blue eyes, short hair, and a figure that had once been stunning, and was now shot. The hour glass had become an accordion, or so she had told Sheila. She wore gray sweats and walked around barefoot.

Her father, Gary, had lost much of his blond hair, and had resorted to allowing it to grow long so that he could flop it over on one side to cover his baldness. His face was sturdy, and might have been considered handsome, if it was not-so-thoroughly average. His jacket had been draped on the back of his chair and his red "power tie" hung loosely around his neck, slicing into the field of his crisp white shirt like a blood stain.

Soon the meal was finished and Sheila offered to clear. She saw the way her parents were staring at each other and wanted to be as far away as possible when the explosion erupted. As it turned out, she was in the kitchen, washing off the dishes, when the angry screams began. Sheila put down the plate she had been holding and went to the barroom style slatted double doors. She peeked through one corner and saw her parents gesturing wildly with their hands.

"You don't *know* that," Gary hollered.

"Fine, I don't know anything, do I? You're the smart one. You're the one with all the answers. I'm just the bimbo who fell in love with you and gave up her dreams so that you could go after yours. Not that anything I've done counts for anything."

"We are seventy-one *thousand* dollars in debt, Colleen. I didn't see you complaining every time we went out to a fancy restaurant. I didn't hear you telling me not to buy all that crap you said we needed over the years. All the clothes, all the furniture—"

"Yeah, right, I'm at fault for wanting to feed and clothe our family. We should have gone naked and ate crumbs off the floor. Gimme a break. Like I'm the one who had to have the Porsche that was in the shop twice a week for five years. I'm the one who had to buy at least two of every new stereo component, VCR, and whatever-the-hell-else just because it was there. I'm the one that if something broke, instead of trying to fix it, I'd pile it in the corner and buy a new one, then lose the receipt so that we couldn't get it serviced, even if we wanted to.

"You're right, Gary. That's the important stuff. That's the essentials. Hell, we could have just gotten rid of the house and lived in the Porsche, couldn't we? I mean, that's the way to create a stable home environment for our daughter, right?"

Standing at the door, Sheila suddenly felt her stomach muscles tighten.

"Don't bring her into this," Gary said. "This isn't about her."

"No? Well, maybe it should be. Don't you see what this is doing to her? Her grades are slipping. She's getting dark circles under her eyes because she's not sleeping right any more. She spends as little time as possible in this house and I'll tell you, Gary, I don't blame her. I don't blame her for one minute."

"Yeah? So what are you saying?"

"I'm not *saying* anything. It's just that we're not going to have the money to put her through college like we promised. Or did you forget that we tapped her college fund last summer just to keep the household going? You said it was just until you got a better job. Just until things turned around and really got going for you, that's what you said."

"So what am I supposed to do? Haven't you seen the news? The economy's in the toilet. We're lucky we have jobs at all," replied Sheila's father.

"Yeah, sure. This is exactly what I wanted to do with my B.A. in business administration. Clean offices in the middle of the night. Take care of watering plants during the day."

"The firm is talking about expanding, about opening an office in the city. Advertising's a tough field, but I've managed to stay in it for twenty years. That counts for something. If the New York office happens, I've been told I'm first in line to head it up."

"Yeah, right. How many times have we heard that? Every time you're up for a promotion, they give it to some new guy, some fresh guy, some *young* guy—"

"Thanks, Colleen, thanks. I really appreciate being reminded of that."

"I'm just saying that right now, if we were a real two income family, maybe we wouldn't be in this kind of trouble. If I could have finished graduate school instead of taking work as a secretary—"

"Hey, you could have gone back to school at any time. No one was stopping you."

"Right. And who was going to raise Sheila? You? What a joke. You can't even take care of yourself. I'm telling you, Gary, things are going to have to level out. I'm really tired of living on this roller coaster."

"So what do you want me to do, huh? What is

it you want? You want to stop the ride and get off?"

"Maybe that's not such a bad idea."

"Any time."

"Yeah, right. Look, just leave me alone, all right? I don't want to deal with this any more tonight. Just leave me alone so I can try and think. It would be so nice just to have some peace and quiet so I could *think* for a change."

Sheila watched as they stared at one another again. Her father broke the silence:

"I'm going out."

"Fine," Colleen said. "You do that."

Sheila turned away from the door and went back to the dishes. Somehow, she had to keep herself from crying. She couldn't let her mother know that she was listening.

Colleen came in. "Why don't you go on, honey. I'll finish up here. I need something to do."

Sheila nodded, afraid to speak, terrified that if she tried, she would end up in her own shouting match with her mother. Instead, she wiped her hands and hurriedly left the kitchen. She went upstairs, to her bedroom, and locked the door behind herself. Sliding down the back of the door, her hands covering her face, she allowed herself the luxury of tears. Deep, wracking sobs were called forth so forcefully that they caused the agony of the soul to which she had become accustomed to surface again.

She didn't want to be here. She didn't want this to be her life. Though she loved both her parents, she didn't know how much more of this she could take.

Finally, when the worst of her tears had been torn from her, Sheila rose and walked to her dresser, and yanked a handful of tissues from the dispenser. Sitting beside the tissue holder was the glorious prize she had bought over the weekend. Sheila blew her nose, took some more tissues, cleaned herself up, then lifted the mask.

When she touched it, she felt a slight, electric shock, a strange vibration, as if it were charged with the magic of infinite dreams and possibilities. The mask was more beautiful than she had remembered. The face plate was made of a strange white lace so fine that it was almost transparent. The material alone shouldn't have been strong enough to hold the molded features of a startlingly beautiful woman, but the fabric had been treated with some substance that held it in shape.

Upon the face plate lay fantastic designs of midnight blue, emerald green, sparkling gold, and bloody crimson. They spiraled and danced upon the surface of the mask as Sheila turned it this way and that, fascinated by the trick of the light that made the designs appear to shift and metamorphose. Strands of fabric created laser thin feathers that reached out from the eyebrows, and the crown of the mask, meant for holding a long, lustrous collection of hair, was a strange yet lovely design that might have come from ancient Egypt or some mysterious, forgotten culture. At its center lay an inverted ankh, symbolizing enduring life, and surrounding that were several tiers of wraithlike figures straining heavenbound, reaching for an altar made of swords.

The mask had set Sheila back six dollars.

She thought of all the horrible things her parents had said to one another and wished desperately for some way to escape. The mask tingled even more violently. She raised it to her face, wondering if she would even be able to see out of it, and pulled the silk cord out so that she could slip it over her head. The surface of the mask pressed against her bare flesh with startling speed. The ferocity of the pressure felt like a thousand needles suddenly coming to life.

Without warning, a fiery hand reached into her brain. Colors exploded before her eyes. She wanted to scream, she wanted to get help, but it was too late.

The world suddenly vanished and darkness became her entire existence.

**Look for *Nightmare Club* #4, *The Mask*
by Nick Baron
Coming in September 1993.**

a "suicide" pact, they sign their names in blood, vowing to kill themselves to keep the depot intact. Of course, they never really intend to carry out the pact . . .

Then, one by one, those who signed the blood pact, begin to die. The deaths are labeled suicides, but Jamie suspects her friends are really being murdered. Now she must unmask a cunning killer who's watching *her* every move. If she doesn't, she'll be the next to die!

DEADLY DELIVERY by Michael August

It's just another long, hot summer—until Derek Cliver and his friends join an exciting new mail-order club. The Terror Club allows Derek and his friends to create their own monsters. *And* it gives them the opportunity to "dispose" of those they despise most. But the game turns terrifyingly real when the monsters they create come to life—and actually murder their rivals.

Now, as the body count rises, Derek and his friends must somehow undo what they've done . . . before they become the next victims!

You can become a
member of

We dare you to join THE NIGHT-
MARE CLUB...and receive your
special member's packet including your
membership card, THE NIGHTMARE
CLUB Newsletter, a poster of THE
NIGHTMARE CLUB insignia, auto-
graphed photos of the authors, and
other exciting gifts.

To join, send your name and address to:

The Nightmare Club
Membership Dept.
Z*Fave Books
475 Park Avenue South
New York, NY 10016

Please allow 6–8 weeks for delivery.
Quantities limited. Offer good while supplies last.